D1095556

THE LEANING TOWER
AND OTHER STORIES

by the same author

FLOWERING JUDAS
AND OTHER STORIES

PALE HORSE, PALE RIDER

KATHERINE ANNE PORTER

THE LEANING TOWER

AND OTHER STORIES

hb

HARCOURT, BRACE AND COMPANY, NEW YORK

[b·9·44]

A WARTIME BOOK

This complete edition is produced in full compliance with the government's regulations for conserving paper and other essential materials.

PRINTED IN THE UNITED STATES OF AMERICA

To Corporal Harrison Paul Porter, Jr.

CONTENTS

THE SOURCE

The Source

ONCE a year, in early summer, after school was closed and the children were to be sent to the farm, the Grandmother began to long for the country. With an air of tenderness, as if she enquired after a favorite child, she would ask questions about the crops, wonder what kind of gardens the Negroes were making, how the animals were faring. She would remark now and then, "I begin to feel the need of a little change and relaxation, too," in a vague tone of reassurance, as if to say this did not mean that she intended for a moment really to relax her firm hold on family affairs. It was her favorite theory that change of occupation was one way, probably the best way, of resting. The three grandchildren would begin to feel the faint sure stirrings of departure in the house; her son, their father, would assume the air of careful patience which imperfectly masked his annoyance at the coming upsets and inconveniences to be endured at the farm. "Now, Harry, now, Harry!" his mother would warn him, for she was never deceived by his manner; indeed, he never meant her to be; and she would begin trying to placate him by wondering falsely if she could possibly get away, after all, with so much yet to be done where she was. She looked forward with pleasure to a breath of country air. She always imagined herself as walking at leisure in the shade of the orchards watching the peaches ripen; she spoke with longing of clipping the rosebushes, or of tying up the trellised honeysuckle with her own hands. She would pack up her summer-weight black skirts, her thin black-and-white basques, and would get out a broad-brimmed, rather battered straw shepherdess hat she had woven for herself just after the War. Trying it on, turning her head critically this way and that before the mirror, she would decide that it might do nicely for the sun and she always took it along, but never wore it. She wore instead a stiffly starched white chambray bonnet, with a round crown buttoned on a narrow brim; it sat pertly on the top of her head with a fly-away look, the long strings hanging stiffly. Underneath this head-dress, her pale, tightly drawn, very old face looked out with stately calm.

In the early spring, when the Indian cling peach-tree against the wall of the town house began to bloom, she would say, "I have planted five orchards in three States, and now I see only one tree in bloom." A soft, enjoyable melancholy would come over her; she would stand quite still for a moment looking at the single tree, representing all her beloved trees still blooming, flourishing, and preparing to bring forth fruit in their separate places.

Leaving Aunt Nannie, who had been nurse to her children, in charge of the town house, she set out on her journey.

If departure was a delightful adventure for the children, arriving at the farm was an event for Grandmother. Hinry came running to open the gate, his coal-black face burst into a grin, his voice flying before him: "Howdy-do, Miss Sophia Jane!", simply not noticing that the carry-all was spilling over with other members of the family. The horses jogged in, their bellies jolting and churning, and Grandmother, calling out greetings in her feast-day voice, alighted, surrounded by her people, with the same flurry of travel that marked her journeys by train; but now with an indefinable sense of homecoming, not to the house but to the black, rich soft land and the human beings living on it. Without removing her long veiled widow's bonnet, she would walk straight through the house, observing instantly that everything was out of order; pass out into the yards and gardens, silently glancing, making instant plans for changes; down the narrow path past the barns, with a glance into and around them as she went, a glance of firm and purposeful censure; and on past the canebrake to the left, the hayfields to the right, until she arrived at the row of Negro huts that ran along the bois d'arc hedge.

Stepping up with a pleasant greeting to all, which in no

way promised exemption from the wrath to come, she went into their kitchens, glanced into their meal barrels, their ovens, their cupboard shelves, into every smallest crevice and corner, with Littie and Dicey and Hinry and Bumper and Keg following, trying to explain that things was just a little out of shape right now because they'd had so much outside work they hadn't just been able to straighten out the way they meant to; but they were going to get at it right away.

Indeed they were, as Grandmother well knew. Within an hour someone would have driven away in the buckboard with an order for such lime for whitewash, so many gallons of kerosene oil, and so much carbolic acid and insect powder. Home-made lye soap would be produced from the wash-house, and the frenzy would begin. Every mattress cover was emptied of its corn husks and boiled, every little Negro on the place was set to work picking a fresh supply of husks, every hut was thickly whitewashed, bins and cupboards were scrubbed, every chair and bedstead was varnished, every filthy quilt was brought to light, boiled in a great iron wash-pot and stretched in the sun; and the uproar had all the special character of any annual occasion. The Negro women were put at making a fresh supply of shirts for the men and children, cotton dresses and aprons for themselves. Whoever wished to complain now seized his opportunity. Mister Harry had clean forgot to buy shoes for Hinry, look at Hinry: Hinry had been just like that, barefooted the live-long winter. Mister Miller (a red-whiskered man who occupied a dubious situation somewhere between overseer when Mister Harry was absent, and plain hired hand when he was present) had skimped them last winter on everything you could think of—not enough cornmeal, not half enough bacon, not enough wood, not enough of anything. Littie had needed a little sugar for her cawfy and do you think Mister Miller would let her have it? No. Mister Miller had said nobody needed sugar in their cawfy. Hinry said Mister Miller didn't even take sugar in his own cawfy because he was just too stingy. Boosker, the three-year-old baby, had earache in January and Miz Carleton had come down and put lodnum in it and Boosker was acting like she was deef ever since. The black horse Mister Harry bought last fall had gone clean wild and jumped a barbed wire fence and tore his chest almost off and hadn't been any good from that time on.

All these annoyances and dozens like them had to be soothed at once, then Grandmother's attention was turned to the main house, which must be overhauled completely. The big secretaries were opened and shabby old sets of Dickens, Scott, Thackeray, Dr. Johnson's dictionary, the volumes of Pope and Milton and Dante and Shakespeare were dusted off and closed up carefully again. Curtains came down in dingy heaps and went up again stiff and sweet-smelling; rugs were heaved forth in dusty confusion and returned flat and gay with flowers once more; the kitchen was no longer dingy and desolate but a place of heavenly order where it was tempting to linger.

Next the barns and smokehouses and the potato cellar, the gardens and every tree or vine or bush must have that restoring touch upon it. For two weeks this would go on, with the Grandmother a tireless, just and efficient slave driver of every creature on the place. The children ran wild outside, but not as they did when she was not there. The hour came in each day when they were rounded up, captured, washed, dressed properly, made to eat what was set before them without giving battle, put to bed when the time came and no nonsense . . . They loved their Grandmother; she was the only reality to them in a world that seemed otherwise without fixed authority or refuge, since their mother had died so early that only the eldest girl remembered her vaguely: just the same they felt that Grandmother was tyrant, and they wished to be free of her; so they were always pleased when, on a certain day, as a sign that her visit was drawing to an end, she would go out to the pasture and call her old saddle horse, Fiddler.

He had been a fine, thorough-paced horse once, but he was now a weary, disheartened old hero, gray-haired on his jaw and chin, who spent his life nuzzling with pendulous lips for tender bits of grass or accepting sugar cautiously between his shaken teeth. He paid no attention to anyone but the Grandmother. Every summer when she went to his field and called him, he came doddering up with almost a gleam in his filmy eyes. The two old creatures would greet each other fondly. The Grandmother always treated her animal friends as if they were human beings temporarily metamorphosed, but not by this accident dispensed from those duties suitable to their condition. She would have Fiddler brought around under her old side-saddle—her little granddaughters rode astride and she saw no harm in it, for them—and mount with her foot in Uncle Jimbilly's curved hand. Fiddler would remember his youth and break into a stiff-legged gallop, and off she would go with her crepe bands and her old-fashioned riding skirt flying. They always returned at a walk, the Grandmother sitting straight as a sword, smiling, triumphant. Dismounting at the horse-block by herself, she would stroke Fiddler on the neck before turning him over to Uncle Jimbilly, and walk away carrying her train grandly over her arm.

This yearly gallop with Fiddler was important to her; it proved her strength, her unabated energy. Any time now Fiddler might drop in his tracks, but she would not. She would say, "He's getting stiff in the knees," or "He's pretty short-winded this year," but she herself walked lightly and breathed as easily as ever, or so she chose to believe.

That same afternoon or the next day, she would take her long-promised easy stroll in the orchards with nothing to do, her Grandchildren running before her and running back to her side: with nothing at all to do, her hands folded, her skirts trailing and picking up twigs, turning over little stones, sweeping a faint path behind her, her white bonnet askew over one eye, an absorbed fixed smile on her lips, her eyes missing nothing. This walk would usually end with Hinry or Jimbilly being dispatched to the orchards at once to make some trifling but indispensable improvement.

It would then come over her powerfully that she was staying on idling when there was so much to be done at home . . . There would be a last look at everything, instructions, advices, good-bys, blessings. She would set out with that strange look of leaving forever, and arrive at the place in town with the same air of home-coming she had worn on her arrival in the country, in a gentle flurry of greeting and felicitations, as if she had been gone for half a year. At once she set to work restoring to order the place which no doubt had gone somewhat astray in her absence.

THE WITNESS

The Witness

UNCLE JIMBILLY was so old and had spent so many years bowed over things, putting them together and taking them apart, making them over and making them do, he was bent almost double. His hands were closed and stiff from gripping objects tightly, while he worked at them, and they could not open altogether even if a child took the thick black fingers and tried to turn them back. He hobbled on a stick; his purplish skull showed through patches in his wool, which had turned greenish gray and looked as if the moths had got at it.

He mended harness and put half soles on the other Negroes' shoes, he built fences and chicken coops and barn doors; he stretched wires and put in new window panes and fixed sagging hinges and patched up roofs; he repaired carriage tops and cranky plows. Also he had a gift for carving miniature tombstones out of blocks of wood; give him almost any kind of piece of wood and he could turn out a tombstone, shaped very like the real ones, with carving, and a name and date on it if they were needed. They were often needed, for some small beast or bird was always dying and having to be buried with proper ceremonies: the cart draped as a hearse, a shoe-box coffin with a pall over it, a profuse floral outlay, and, of course, a tombstone. As he worked, turning the long blade of his bowie knife deftly in circles to cut a flower, whittling and smoothing the back and sides, stopping now and then to hold it at arm's length and examine it with one eye closed, Uncle Jimbilly would talk in a low, broken, abstracted murmur, as if to himself; but he was really saying something he meant one to hear. Sometimes it would be an incomprehensible ghost story; listen ever so carefully, at the end it was impossible to decide whether Uncle Jimbilly himself had seen the ghost, whether it was a real ghost at all, or only another man dressed like one; and he dwelt much on the horrors of slave times.

"Dey used to take 'em out and tie 'em down and whup 'em," he muttered, "wid gret big leather strops inch thick long as yo' ahm, wid round holes bored in 'em so's evey time dey hit 'em de hide and de meat done come off dey bones in little round chunks. And wen dey had whupped 'em wid de strop till dey backs was all raw and bloody, dey spread dry cawnshucks on dey backs and set 'em afire and pahched 'em, and den dey poured vinega all ovah 'em . . . Yassuh. And den, the ve'y nex day dey'd got to git back to work in the fiels or dey'd do the same thing right ovah agin. Yassah. Dat was it. If dey didn't git back to work dey got it all right ovah agin."

The children—three of them: a serious, prissy older girl

of ten, a thoughtful sad looking boy of eight, and a quick flighty little girl of six—sat disposed around Uncle Jimbilly and listened with faint tinglings of embarrassment. They knew, of course, that once upon a time Negroes had been slaves; but they had all been freed long ago and were now only servants. It was hard to realize that Uncle Jimbilly had been born in slavery, as the Negroes were always saying. The children thought that Uncle Jimbilly had got over his slavery very well. Since they had known him, he had never done a single thing that anyone told him to do. He did his work just as he pleased and when he pleased. If you wanted a tombstone, you had to be very careful about the way you asked for it. Nothing could have been more impersonal and faraway than his tone and manner of talking about slavery, but they wriggled a little and felt guilty. Paul would have changed the subject, but Miranda, the little quick one, wanted to know the worst. "Did they act like that to you, Uncle Jimbilly?" she asked.

"No, *mam*," said Uncle Jimbilly. "Now whut name you want on dis one? Dey nevah did. Dey done 'em dat way in the rice swamps. I always worked right here close to the house or in town with Miss Sophia. Down in the swamps . . ."

"Didn't they ever die, Uncle Jimbilly?" asked Paul.

"Cose dey died," said Uncle Jimbilly, "cose dey died—

dey died," he went on, pursing his mouth gloomily, "by de thousands and tens upon thousands."

"Can you carve 'Safe in Heaven' on that, Uncle Jimbilly?" asked Maria in her pleasant, mincing voice.

"To put over a tame jackrabbit, Missy?" asked Uncle Jimbilly indignantly. He was very religious. "A heathen like dat? No, *mam.* In de swamps dey used to stake 'em out all day and all night, and all day and all night and all day wid dey hans and feet tied so dey couldn't scretch and let de muskeeters eat 'em alive. De muskeeters 'ud bite 'em tell dey was all swole up like a balloon all over, and you could heah em howlin and prayin all ovah the swamp. Yassuh. Dat was it. And nary a drop of watah noh a moufful of braid . . . Yassuh, dat's it. Lawd, dey done it. Hosanna! Now take dis yere tombstone and don' bother me no more . . . or I'll . . ."

Uncle Jimbilly was apt to be suddenly annoyed and you never knew why. He was easily put out about things, but his threats were always so exorbitant that not even the most credulous child could be terrified by them. He was always going to do something quite horrible to somebody and then he was going to dispose of the remains in a revolting manner. He was going to skin somebody alive and nail the hide on the barn door, or he was just getting ready to cut off somebody's ears with a hatchet and pin them on Bongo, the crop-eared brindle dog. He was often all prepared in his mind to pull somebody's teeth and make a set of false teeth for Ole Man Ronk . . . Ole Man Ronk was a tramp who had been living all summer in the little cabin behind the smokehouse. He got his rations along with the Negroes and sat all day mumbling his naked gums. He had skimpy black whiskers which appeared to be set in wax, and angry red eyelids. He took morphine, it was said; but what morphine might be, or how he took it, or why, no one seemed to know . . . Nothing could have been more unpleasant than the notion that one's teeth might be given to Ole Man Ronk.

The reason why Uncle Jimbilly never did any of these things he threatened was, he said, because he never could get round to them. He always had so much other work on hand he never seemed to get caught up on it. But some day, somebody was going to get a mighty big surprise, and meanwhile everybody had better look out.

THE CIRCUS

The Circus

THE long planks set on trestles rose one above the other to a monstrous height and stretched dizzyingly in a wide oval ring. They were packed with people—"lak fleas on a dog's ear," said Dicey, holding Miranda's hand firmly and looking about her with disapproval. The white billows of enormous canvas sagged overhead, held up by three poles set evenly apart down the center. The family, when seated, occupied almost a whole section on one level.

On one side of them in a long row sat Father, sister Maria, brother Paul, Grandmother; great-aunt Keziah, cousin Keziah, and second-cousin Keziah, who had just come down from Kentucky on a visit; uncle Charles Breaux, cousin Charles Breaux, and aunt Marie-Anne Breaux. On the other side sat small cousin Lucie Breaux, big cousin Paul Gay, great-aunt Sally Gay (who took snuff and was therefore a disgrace to the family); two strange, extremely handsome young men who might be cousins but who were certainly in love with cousin Miranda Gay; and cousin Miranda Gay herself, a most dashing young lady with crisp silk skirts, a half dozen of them at once, a lovely perfume and wonderful black curly hair above enormous wild gray eyes, "like a colt's," Father said. Miranda hoped to be exactly like her when she grew up. Hanging to Dicey's arm she leaned out and waved to cousin Miranda, who waved back smiling, and the strange young men waved to her also. Miranda was most fearfully excited. It was her first circus; it might also be her last because the whole family had combined to persuade Grandmother to allow her to come with them. "Very well, this once," Grandmother said, "since it's a family reunion."

This once! This once! She could not look hard enough at everything. She even peeped down between the wide crevices of the piled-up plank seats, where she was astonished to see odd-looking, roughly dressed little boys peeping up from the dust below. They were squatted in little heaps, staring up quietly. She looked squarely into the eyes of one, who returned her a look so peculiar she gazed and gazed, trying to understand it. It was a bold grinning stare without any kind of friendliness in it. He was a thin, dirty little boy with a floppy old checkerboard cap pulled over crumpled red ears and dust-colored hair. As she gazed he nudged the little boy next to him, whispered, and the second little boy caught her eye. This was too much. Miranda pulled Dicey's sleeve. "Dicey, what are those little boys doing down there?" "Down where?" asked Dicey, but she seemed to know already, for she bent over and looked through the crevice, drew her knees together and her skirts around her, and said severely: "You jus mind yo' own business and stop throwin' yo' legs around that way. Don't you pay any mind. Plenty o' monkeys right here in the show widout you studyin dat kind."

An enormous brass band seemed to explode right at Miranda's ear. She jumped, quivered, thrilled blindly and almost forgot to breathe as sound and color and smell rushed together and poured through her skin and hair and beat in her head and hands and feet and pit of her stomach. "Oh," she called out in her panic, closing her eyes and seizing Dicey's hand hard. The flaring lights burned through her lids, a roar of laughter like rage drowned out the steady raging of the drums and horns. She opened her eyes . . . A creature in a blousy white overall with ruffles at the neck and ankles, with bone-white skull and chalk-white face, with tufted eyebrows far apart in the middle of his forehead, the lids in a black sharp angle, a long scarlet mouth stretching back into sunken cheeks, turned up at the corners in a perpetual bitter grimace of pain, astonishment, not smiling, pranced along a wire stretched down the center of the ring, balancing a long thin pole with little wheels at either end. Miranda thought at first he was walking on air, or flying, and this did not surprise her; but when she saw the wire, she was terrified. High above their heads the inhuman figure pranced, spinning the little wheels. He paused, slipped, the flapping white leg waved in space; he staggered, wobbled, slipped sidewise, plunged, and caught the wire with frantic knee, hanging there upside down, the other leg waving like a feeler above his head; slipped once more, caught by one frenzied heel, and swung back and forth like a scarf . . . The crowd roared with savage delight, shrieks of dreadful laughter like devils in delicious torment . . . Miranda shrieked too, with real pain, clutching at her stomach with her knees drawn up . . . The man on the wire, hanging by his foot, turned his head like a seal from side to side and blew sneering kisses from his cruel mouth. Then Miranda covered her eyes and screamed, the tears pouring over her cheeks and chin.

"Take her home," said her father, "get her out of here at once," but the laughter was not wiped from his face. He merely glanced at her and back to the ring. "Take her away, Dicey," called the Grandmother, from under her half-raised crepe veil. Dicey, rebelliously, very slowly, without taking her gaze from the white figure swaying on the wire, rose, seized the limp, suffering bundle, prodded and lumped her way over knees and feet, through the crowd, down the levels of the scaffolding, across a space of sandy tanbark, out through a flap in the tent. Miranda was crying steadily with an occasional hiccough. A dwarf was standing in the entrance, wearing a little woolly beard, a pointed cap, tight red breeches, long shoes with turned-up toes. He carried a thin white wand. Miranda almost touched him before she saw him, her distorted face with its open mouth and glistening tears almost level with his. He leaned forward and peered at her with kind, not-human golden eyes, like a near-sighted dog: then made a horrid grimace at her, imitating her own face. Miranda struck at him in sheer ill temper, screaming. Dicey drew her away quickly, but not before Miranda had seen in his face, suddenly, a look of haughty, remote displeasure, a true grown-up look. She knew it well. It chilled her with a new kind of fear: she had not believed he was really human.

"Raincheck, get your raincheck!" said a very disagreeable looking fellow as they passed. Dicey turned toward him almost in tears herself. "Mister, caint you see I won't be able to git back? I got this young un to see to . . . What good dat lil piece of paper goin to do *me?*" All the way home she was cross, and grumbled under her breath: little ole meany . . . little ole scare-cat . . . gret big baby . . . never go nowhere . . . never see nothin . . . come on here now, hurry up—always ruinin everything for othah folks . . . won't let anybody rest a minute, won't let anybody have any good times . . . come on here now, you wanted to go home and you're going there . . . snatching Miranda along, vicious but cautious, careful not to cross the line where Miranda could say outright: "Dicey did this or said this to me . . ." Dicey was allowed a certain freedom up to a point.

The family trooped into the house just before dark and scattered out all over it. From every room came the sound of chatter and laughter. The other children told Miranda what she had missed: wonderful little ponies with plumes and bells on their bridles, ridden by darling little monkeys in velvet jackets and peaked hats . . . trained white goats that danced . . . a baby elephant that crossed his front feet and leaned against his cage and opened his mouth to be fed, *such* a baby! . . . more clowns, funnier than the first one even . . . beautiful ladies with bright yellow hair, wearing white silk tights with red satin sashes had performed on white trapezes; they also had hung by their toes, but how gracefully, like flying birds! Huge white horses had lolloped around and round the ring with men and women dancing on their backs! One man had swung by his teeth from the top of the tent and another had put his head in a lion's mouth. Ah, what she had not missed! Everybody had been enjoying themselves while she was missing her first big circus and spoiling the day for Dicey. Poor Dicey. Poor dear Dicey. The other children who hadn't thought of Dicey until that moment, mourned over her with sad mouths, their malicious eyes watching Miranda squirm. Dicey had been looking forward for weeks to this day! And then Miranda must get scared—"Can you *imagine* being afraid of that funny old clown?" each one asked the other, and then they smiled pityingly on Miranda . . .

Then too, it had been a very important occasion in another way: it was the first time Grandmother had ever allowed herself to be persuaded to go to the circus. One could not gather, from her rather generalized opinions, whether there had been no circuses when she was young, or there had been and it was not proper to see them. At any rate for her usual sound reasons, Grandmother had never approved of circuses, and though she would not deny she had been amused somewhat, still there had been sights and sounds in this one which she maintained were, to say the least, not particularly edifying to the young. Her son Harry, who came in while the children made an early supper, looked at their illuminated faces, all the brothers and sisters and visiting cousins, and said, "This basket of young doesn't seem to be much damaged." His mother said, "The fruits of their present are in a future so far off, neither of us may live to know whether harm has been done or not. That is the trouble," and she went on ladling out hot milk to pour over their buttered toast. Miranda was sitting silent, her underlip drooping. Her father smiled at her. "You missed it, Baby," he said softly, "and what good did that do you?"

Miranda burst again into tears: had to be taken away at last, and her supper was brought up to her. Dicey was exasperated and silent. Miranda could not eat. She tried, as if she were really remembering them, to think of the beautiful wild beings in white satin and spangles and red sashes who danced and frolicked on the trapezes; of the sweet little furry ponies and the lovely pet monkeys in their comical clothes. She fell asleep, and her invented memories gave way before her real ones, the bitter terrified face of the man in blowsy white falling to his death—ah, the cruel joke!—and the terrible grimace of the unsmiling dwarf. She screamed in her sleep and sat up crying for deliverance from her torments.

Dicey came, her cross, sleepy eyes half-closed, her big dark mouth pouted, thumping the floor with her thick bare feet. "I *swear,*" she said, in a violent hoarse whisper. "What the matter with you? You need a good spankin, I *swear!* Wakin everybody up like this . . ."

Miranda was completely subjugated by her fears. She had a way of answering Dicey back. She would say, "Oh, hush up, Dicey." Or she would say, "I don't have to mind *you.* I don't have to mind anybody but my grandmother," which was provokingly true. And she would say, "You don't know what you're talking about." The day just past had changed that. Miranda sincerely did not want anybody, not even Dicey, to be cross with her. Ordinarily she did not care how cross she made the harassed adults around her. Now if Dicey must be cross, she still did not really care, if only Dicey might not turn out the lights and leave her to the fathomless terrors of the darkness where sleep could overtake her once more. She hugged Dicey with both arms, crying, "Don't, don't leave me. *Don't* be so angry! I c-c-can't b-bear it!"

Dicey lay down beside her with a long moaning sigh, which meant that she was collecting her patience and making up her mind to remember that she was a Christian and must bear her cross. "Now you go to sleep," she said, in her usual warm being-good voice. "Now you jes shut yo eyes and go to sleep. I ain't going to leave you. Dicey ain't mad at nobody . . . *no*body in the whole worl' . . ."

THE OLD ORDER

The Old Order

IN their later years, the Grandmother and old Nannie used to sit together for some hours every day over their sewing. They shared a passion for cutting scraps of the family finery, hoarded for fifty years, into strips and triangles, and fitting them together again in a carefully disordered patchwork, outlining each bit of velvet or satin or taffeta with a running briar stitch in clear lemon-colored silk floss. They had contrived enough bed and couch covers, table spreads, dressing table scarfs, to have furnished forth several households. Each piece as it was finished was lined with yellow silk, folded, and laid away in a chest, never again to see the light of day. The Grandmother was the great-granddaughter of Kentucky's most famous pioneer: he had, while he was surveying Kentucky, hewed out rather competently a rolling pin for his wife. This rolling pin was the Grandmother's irreplaceable treasure. She covered it with an extraordinarily complicated bit of patchwork, added golden tassels to the handles, and hung it in a conspicuous place in her room. She was the daughter of a notably heroic captain in the War of 1812. She had his razors in a shagreen case and a particularly severe-looking daguerreotype taken in his old age, with his chin in a tall stock and his black satin waistcoat smoothed over a still-handsome military chest. So she fitted a patchwork case over the shagreen and made a sort of envelope of cut velvet and violet satin, held together with briar stitching, to contain the portrait. The rest of her handiwork she put away, to the relief of her grandchildren, who had arrived at the awkward age when Grandmother's quaint old-fashioned ways caused them acute discomfort.

In the summer the women sat under the mingled trees of the side garden, which commanded a view of the east wing, the front and back porches, a good part of the front garden and a corner of the small fig grove. Their choice of this location was a part of their domestic strategy. Very little escaped them: a glance now and then would serve to keep them fairly well informed as to what was going on in the whole place. It is true they had not seen Miranda the day she pulled up the whole mint bed to give to a pleasant strange young woman who stopped and asked her for a sprig of fresh mint. They had never found out who stole the giant pomegranates growing too near the fence: they had not been in time to stop Paul from setting himself on fire while experimenting with a miniature blowtorch, but they had been on the scene to extinguish him with rugs, to pour oil on him, and lecture him. They never saw Maria climbing trees, a mania she had to indulge or pine away, for she chose tall ones on the opposite side of the house. But such casualties were so minor a part of the perpetual round of events that they did not feel defeated nor that their strategy was a failure. Summer, in many ways so desirable a season, had its drawbacks. The children were everywhere at once and the Negroes loved lying under the hackberry grove back of the barns playing seven-up, and eating watermelons. The summer house was in a small town a few miles from the farm, a compromise between the rigorously ordered house in the city and the sprawling old farmhouse which Grandmother had built with such pride and pains. It had, she often said, none of the advantages of either country or city, and all the discomforts of both. But the children loved it.

During the winters in the city, they sat in Grandmother's room, a large squarish place with a small coal grate. All the sounds of life in the household seemed to converge there, echo, retreat, and return. Grandmother and Aunt Nannie knew the whole complicated code of sounds, could interpret and comment on them by an exchange of glances, a lifted eyebrow, or a tiny pause in their talk.

They talked about the past, really—always about the past. Even the future seemed like something gone and done with when they spoke of it. It did not seem an extension of their past, but a repetition of it. They would agree that nothing remained of life as they had known it, the world was changing swiftly, but by the mysterious logic of hope they insisted that each change was probably the last; or if not, a series of changes might bring them, blessedly, back full-circle to the old ways they had known. Who knows why they loved their past? It had been bitter for them both, they had questioned the burdensome rule they lived by every day of their lives, but without rebellion and without expecting an answer. This unbroken thread of inquiry in their minds contained no doubt as to the utter rightness and justice of the basic laws of human existence, founded as they were on God's plan; but they wondered perpetually, with only a hint now and then to each other of the uneasiness of their hearts, how so much suffering and confusion could have been built up and maintained on such a foundation. The Grandmother's rôle was authority, she knew that; it was her duty to portion out activities, to urge or restrain where necessary, to teach morals, manners, and religion, to punish and reward her own household according to a fixed code. Her own doubts and hesitations she concealed, also, she reminded herself, as a matter of duty. Old Nannie had no ideas at all as to her place in the world. It had been assigned to her before birth, and for her daily rule she had all her life obeyed the authority nearest to her.

So they talked about God, about heaven, about planting a new hedge of rose bushes, about the new ways of preserving fruit and vegetables, about eternity and their mutual hope that they might pass it happily together, and often a scrap of silk under their hands would start them on long trains of family reminiscences. They were always amused to notice again how the working of their memories differed in such important ways. Nannie could recall names to perfection; she could always say what the weather had been like on all important occasions, what certain ladies had worn, how handsome certain gentlemen had been, what there had been to eat and drink. Grandmother had masses of dates in her mind, and no memories attached to them: her memories of events seemed detached and floating beyond time. For example, the 26th of August, 1871, had been some sort of red-letter day for her. She had said to herself then that never would she forget that date; and indeed, she remembered it well, but she no longer had the faintest notion what had happened to stamp it on her memory. Nannie was no help in the matter; she had nothing to do with dates. She did not know the year of her birth, and would never have had a birthday to celebrate if Grandmother had not, when she was still Miss Sophia Jane, aged ten, opened a calendar at random, closed her eyes, and marked a date unseen with a pen. So it turned out that Nannie's birthday thereafter fell on June 11, and the year, Miss Sophia Jane decided, should be 1827, her own birth-year, making Nannie just three months younger than her mistress. Sophia Jane then made an entry of Nannie's birth-date in the family Bible, inserting it just below her own. "Nannie Gay," she wrote, in stiff careful letters, "(black)," and though there was some uproar when this was discovered, the ink was long since sunk deeply into the paper, and besides no one was really upset enough to have it scratched out. There it remained, one of their pleasantest points of reference.

They talked about religion, and the slack way the world was going nowadays, the decay of behavior, and about the younger children, whom these topics always brought at once to mind. On these subjects they were firm, critical, and unbewildered. They had received educations which furnished them an assured habit of mind about all the important appearances of life, and especially about the rearing of young. They relied with perfect acquiescence on the dogma that children were conceived in sin and brought forth in iniquity. Childhood was a long state of instruction and probation for adult life, which was in turn a long, severe, undeviating devotion to duty, the largest part of which consisted in bringing up children. The young were difficult, disobedient, and tireless in wrongdoing, apt to turn unkind and undutiful when they grew up, in spite of all one had done for them, or had tried to do: for small painful doubts rose in them now and again when they looked at their completed works. Nannie couldn't abide her new-fangled grandchildren. "Wuthless, shiftless lot, jes plain scum, Miss Sophia Jane; I cain't undahstand it aftah all the raisin' dey had."

The Grandmother defended them, and dispraised her own second generation—heartily, too, for she sincerely found grave faults in them—which Nannie defended in turn. "When they are little, they trample on your feet, and when they grow up they trample on your heart." This was about all there was to say about children in any generation, but the fascination of the theme was endless. They said it thoroughly over and over with thousands of small variations, with always an example among their own friends or family connections to prove it. They had enough material of their own. Grandmother had borne eleven children, Nannie thirteen. They boasted of it. Grandmother would say, "I am the mother of eleven children," in a faintly amazed tone, as if she hardly expected to be believed, or could even quite believe it herself. But she could still point to nine of them. Nannie had lost ten of hers. They were all buried in Kentucky. Nannie never doubted or expected anyone else to doubt she had children. Her boasting was of another order. "Thirteen of 'em," she would say, in an appalled voice, "yas, my Lawd and my Redeemah, thirteen!"

The friendship between the two old women had begun in early childhood, and was based on what seemed even to them almost mythical events. Miss Sophia Jane, a prissy, spoiled five-year-old, with tight black ringlets which were curled every day on a stick, with her stiffly pleated lawn pantalettes and tight bodice, had run to meet her returning father, who had been away buying horses and Negroes. Sitting on his arm, clasping him around the neck, she had watched the wagons filing past on the way to the barns and quarters. On the floor of the first wagon sat two blacks, male and female, holding between them a scrawny, half-naked black child, with a round nubbly head and fixed bright monkey eyes. The baby Negro had a potbelly and her arms were like sticks from wrist to shoulder. She clung with narrow, withered, black leather fingers to her parents, a hand on each.

"I want the little monkey," said Sophia Jane to her father, nuzzling his cheek and pointing. "I want that one to play with."

Behind each wagon came two horses in lead, but in the second wagon there was a small shaggy pony with a thatch of mane over his eyes, a long tail like a brush, a round, hard barrel of a body. He was standing in straw to the knees, braced firmly in a padded stall with a Negro holding his bridle. "Do you see that?" asked her father. "That's for you. High time you learned to ride."

Sophia Jane almost leaped from his arm for joy. She hardly recognized her pony or her monkey the next day, the one clipped and sleek, the other clean in new blue cotton. For a while she could not decide which she loved more, Nannie or Fiddler. But Fiddler did not wear well. She outgrew him in a year, saw him pass without regret to a small brother, though she refused to allow him to be called Fiddler any longer. That name she reserved for a long series of saddle horses. She had named the first in honor of Fiddler Gay, an old Negro who made the music for dances and parties. There was only one Nannie and she outwore Sophia Jane. During all their lives together it was not so much a question of affection between them as a simple matter of being unable to imagine getting on without each other.

Nannie remembered well being on a shallow platform out in front of a great building in a large busy place, the first town she had ever seen. Her father and mother were with her, and there was a thick crowd around them. There were several other small groups of Negroes huddled together with white men bustling them about now and then. She had never seen any of these faces before, and she never saw but one of them again. She remembered it must have been summer, because she was not shivering with cold in her cotton shift. For one thing, her bottom was still burning from a spanking someone (it might have been her mother) had given her just before they got on the platform, to remind her to keep still. Her mother and father were field hands, and had never lived in white folks' houses. A tall gentleman with a long narrow face and very high curved nose, wearing a great-collared blue coat and immensely long light-colored trousers (Nannie could close her eyes and see him again, clearly, as he looked that day) stepped up near them suddenly, while a great hubbub rose. The red-faced man standing on a stump beside them shouted and droned, waving his arms and pointing at Nannie's father and mother. Now and then the tall gentleman raised a finger, without looking at the black people on the platform. Suddenly the shouting died down, the tall gentleman walked over and said to Nannie's father and mother, "Well, Eph! Well, Steeny! Mister Jimmerson comin' to get you in a minute." He poked Nannie in the stomach with a thickly gloved forefinger. "Regular crow-bait," he said to the auctioneer. "I should have had lagniappe with this one."

"A pretty worthless article right now, sir, I agree with you," said the auctioneer, "but it'll grow out of it. As for the team, you won't find a better, I swear."

"I've had an eye on 'em for years," said the tall gentleman, and walked away, motioning as he went to a fat man sitting on a wagon tongue, spitting quantities of tobacco juice. The fat man rose and came over to Nannie and her parents.

Nannie had been sold for twenty dollars: a gift, you might say, hardly sold at all. She learned that a really choice slave sometimes cost more than a thousand dollars. She lived to hear slaves brag about how much they had cost. She had not known how little she fetched on the block until her own mother taunted her with it. This was after Nannie had gone to live for good at the big house, and her mother and father were still in the fields. They lived and worked and died there. A good worming had cured Nannie's potbelly, she thrived on plentiful food and a species of kindness not so indulgent, maybe, as that given to the puppies; still it more than fulfilled her notions of good fortune.

The old women often talked about how strangely things come out in this life. The first owner of Nannie and her parents had gone, Sophia Jane's father said, hog-wild about Texas. It was a new Land of Promise, in 1832. He had sold out his farm and four slaves in Kentucky to raise the money to take a great twenty-mile stretch of land in southwest Texas. He had taken his wife and two young children and set out, and there had been no more news of him for many years. When Grandmother arrived in Texas forty years later, she found him a prosperous ranchman and district judge. Much later, her youngest son met his granddaughter, fell in love with her, and married her—all in three months.

The judge, by then eighty-five years old, was uproarious and festive at the wedding. He reeked of corn liquor, swore by God every other breath, and was rearing to talk about the good old times in Kentucky. The Grandmother showed Nannie to him. "Would you recognize her?" "For God Almighty's sake!" bawled the judge, "is that the strip of crow-bait I sold to your father for twenty dollars? Twenty dollars seemed like a fortune to me in those days!"

While they were jolting home down the steep rocky road on the long journey from San Marcos to Austin, Nannie finally spoke out about her grievance. "Look lak a jedge might had better raisin'," she said, gloomily, "look lak he didn't keer how much he hurt a body's feelins."

The Grandmother, muffled down in the back seat in the corner of the old carryall, in her worn sealskin pelisse, showing coffee-brown at the edges, her eyes closed, her hands wrung together, had been occupied once more in reconciling herself to losing a son, and, as ever, to a girl and a family of which she could not altogether approve. It was not that there was anything seriously damaging to be said against any of them; only—well, she wondered at her sons' tastes. What had each of them in turn found in the wife he had chosen? The Grandmother had always had in mind the kind of wife each of her sons needed; she had tried to bring about better marriages for them than they had made for themselves. They had merely resented her interference in what they considered strictly their personal affairs. She did not realize that she had spoiled and pampered her youngest son until he was in all probability unfit to be any kind of a husband, much less a good one. And there was something about her new daughter-in-law, a tall, handsome, firm-looking young woman, with a direct way of speaking, walking, talking, that seemed to promise that the spoiled Baby's days of clover were ended. The Grandmother was annoyed deeply at seeing how self-possessed the bride had been, how she had had her way about the wedding arrangements down to the last detail, how she glanced now and then at her new husband with calm, humorous, level eyes, as if she had already got him sized up. She had even suggested at the wedding dinner that her idea of a honeymoon would be to follow the chuck-wagon on the round-up, and help in the cattle-branding on her father's ranch. Of course she may have been joking. But she was altogether too Western, too modern, something like the "new" woman who was beginning to run wild, asking for the vote, leaving her home and going out in the world to earn her own living . . .

The Grandmother's narrow body shuddered to the bone at the thought of women so unsexing themselves; she emerged with a start from the dark reverie of foreboding thoughts which left a bitter taste in her throat. "Never mind, Nannie. The judge just wasn't thinking. He's very fond of his good cheer."

Nannie had slept in a bed and had been playmate and work-fellow with her mistress; they fought on almost equal terms, Sophia Jane defending Nannie fiercely against any discipline but her own. When they were both seventeen years old, Miss Sophia Jane was married off in a very gay wedding. The house was jammed to the roof and everybody present was at least fourth cousin to everybody else. There were forty carriages and more than two hundred horses to look after for two days. When the last wheel disappeared down the lane (a number of the guests lingered on for two weeks), the larders and bins were half empty and the place looked as if a troop of cavalry had been over it. A few days later Nannie was married off to a boy she had known ever since she came to the family, and they were given as a wedding present to Miss Sophia Jane.

Miss Sophia Jane and Nannie had then started their grim and terrible race of procreation, a child every sixteen months or so, with Nannie nursing both, and Sophia Jane, in dreadful discomfort, suppressing her milk with bandages and spirits of wine. When they each had produced their fourth child, Nannie almost died of puerperal fever. Sophia Jane nursed both children. She named the black baby Charlie, and her own child Stephen, and she fed them justly turn about, not favoring the white over the black, as Nannie felt obliged to do. Her husband was shocked, tried to forbid her; her mother came to see her and reasoned with her. They found her very difficult and quite stubborn. She had already begun to develop her implicit character, which was altogether just, humane, proud, and simple. She had many small vanities and weaknesses on the surface: a love of luxury and a tendency to resent criticism. This tendency was based on her feeling of superiority in judgment and sensibility to almost everyone around her. It made her very hard to manage. She had a quiet way of holding her ground which convinced her antagonist that she would really die, not just threaten to, rather than give way. She had learned now that she was badly cheated in giving her children to another woman to feed; she resolved never again to be cheated in just that way. She sat nursing her child and her foster child, with a sensual warm pleasure she had not dreamed of, translating her natural physical relief into something holy, God-sent, amends from heaven for what she had suffered in childbed. Yes, and for what she missed in the marriage bed, for there also something had failed. She said to Nannie quite calmly, "From now on, you will nurse your children and I will nurse mine," and it was so. Charlie remained her special favorite among the Negro children. "I understand now," she said to her older sister Keziah, "why the black mammies love their foster children. I love mine." So Charlie was brought up in the house as playmate for her son Stephen, and exempted from hard work all his life.

Sophia Jane had been wooed at arm's length by a mysteriously attractive young man whom she remembered well as rather a snubby little boy with curls like her own, but shorter, a frilled white blouse and kilts of the Macdonald tartan. He was her second cousin and resembled her so closely they had been mistaken for brother and sister. Their grandparents had been first cousins, and sometimes Sophia Jane saw in him, years after they were married, all the faults she had most abhorred in her elder brother: lack of aim, failure to act at crises, a philosophic detachment from practical affairs, a tendency to set projects on foot and then leave them to perish or to be finished by someone else; and a profound conviction that everyone around him should be happy to wait upon him hand and foot. She had fought these fatal tendencies in her brother, within the bounds of wifely prudence she fought them in her husband, she was long after to fight them again in two of her sons and in several of her grandchildren. She gained no victory in any case, the selfish, careless, unloving creatures lived and ended as they had begun. But the Grandmother developed a character truly portentous under the discipline of trying to change the characters of others. Her husband shared with her the family sharpness of eye. He disliked and feared her deadly willfullness, her certainty that her ways were not only right but beyond criticism, that her feelings were important, even in the lightest matter, and must not be tampered with or treated casually. He had disappeared at the critical moment when they were growing up, had gone to college and then for travel; she forgot him for a long time, and when she saw him again forgot him as he had been once for all. She was gay and sweet and decorous, full of vanity and incredibly exalted daydreams which threatened now and again to cast her over the edge of some mysterious forbidden frenzy. She dreamed recurrently that she had lost her virginity (her virtue, she called it), her sole claim to regard, consideration, even to existence, and after frightful moral suffering which masked altogether her physical experience she would wake in a cold sweat, disordered and terrified. She had heard that her cousin Stephen was a little "wild," but that was to be expected. He was leading, no doubt, a dashing life full of manly indulgences, the sweet dark life of the knowledge of evil which caused her hair to crinkle on her scalp when she thought of it. Ah, the delicious, the free, the wonderful, the mysterious and terrible life of men! She thought about it a great deal. "Little day-dreamer," her mother or father would say to her, surprising her in a brown study, eyes moist, lips smiling vaguely over her embroidery or her book, or with hands fallen on her lap, her face turned away to a blank wall. She memorized and saved for these moments scraps of high-minded poetry, which she instantly quoted at them when they offered her a penny for her thoughts; or she broke into a melancholy little song of some kind, a song she knew they liked. She would run to the piano and tinkle the tune out with one hand, saying, "I love this part best," leaving no doubt in their minds as to what her own had been occupied with. She lived her whole youth so, without once giving herself away; not until she was in middle age, her husband dead, her property dispersed, and she found herself with a houseful of children, making a new life for them in another place, with all the responsibilities of a man but with none of the privileges, did she finally emerge into something like an honest life: and yet, she was passionately honest. She had never been anything else.

Sitting under the trees with Nannie, both of them old and their long battle with life almost finished, she said, fingering a scrap of satin, "It was not fair that Sister Keziah should have had this ivory brocade for her wedding dress, and I had only dotted swiss . . ."

"Times was harder when you got married, Missy," said Nannie. "Dat was de yeah all de crops failed."

"And they failed ever afterward, it seems to me," said Grandmother.

"Seems to me like," said Nannie, "dotted swiss was all the style when you got married."

"I never cared for it," said Grandmother.

Nannie, born in slavery, was pleased to think she would not die in it. She was wounded not so much by her state of being as by the word describing it. Emancipation was a sweet word to her. It had not changed her way of living in a single particular, but she was proud of having been able to say to her mistress, "I aim to stay wid you as long as you'll have me." Still, Emancipation had seemed to set right a wrong that stuck in her heart like a thorn. She could not understand why God, Whom she loved, had seen fit to be so hard on a whole race because they had got a certain kind of skin. She talked it over with Miss Sophia Jane. Many times. Miss Sophia Jane was always brisk and opinionated about it:

"Nonsense! I tell you, God does not know whether a skin is black or white. He sees only souls. Don't be getting notions, Nannie—of course you're going to Heaven."

Nannie showed the rudiments of logic in a mind altogether untutored. She wondered, simply and without resentment, whether God, Who had been so cruel to black people on earth, might not continue His severity in the next world. Miss Sophia Jane took pleasure in reassuring her; as if she, who had been responsible for Nannie, body and soul in this life, might also be her sponsor before the judgment seat.

Miss Sophia Jane had taken upon herself all the responsibilities of her tangled world, half white, half black, mingling steadily and the confusion growing ever deeper. There were so many young men about the place, always, younger brothers-in-law, first cousins, second cousins, nephews. They came visiting and they stayed, and there was no accounting for them nor any way of controlling their quietly headstrong habits. She learned early to keep silent and give no sign of uneasiness, but whenever a child was born in the Negro quarters, pink, worm-like, she held her breath for three days, she told her eldest granddaughter, years later, to see whether the newly born would turn black after the proper interval . . . It was a strain that told on her, and ended by giving her a deeply grounded contempt for men. She could not help it, she despised men. She despised them and was ruled by them. Her husband threw away her dowry and her property in wild investments in strange territories: Louisiana, Texas; and without protest she watched him play away her substance like a gambler. She felt that she could have managed her affairs profitably. But her natural activities lay elsewhere, it was the business of a man to make all decisions and dispose of all financial matters. Yet when she got the reins in her hands, her sons could persuade her to this and that enterprise or investment; against her will and judgment she accepted their advice, and among them they managed to break up once more the stronghold she had built for the future of her family. They got from her their own start in life, came back for fresh help when they needed it, and were divided against each other. She saw it as her natural duty to provide for her household, after her husband had fought stubbornly through the War, along with every other man of military age in the connection; had been wounded, had lingered helpless, and had died of his wound long after the great fervor and excitement had faded in hopeless defeat, when to be a man wounded and ruined in the War was merely to have proved oneself, perhaps, more heroic than wise. Left so, she drew her family together and set out for Louisiana, where her husband, with her money, had bought a sugar refinery. There was going to be a fortune in sugar, he said; not in raising the raw material, but in manufacturing it. He had schemes in his head for operating cotton gins, flour mills, refineries. Had he lived . . . but he did not live, and Sophia Jane had hardly repaired the house she bought and got the orchard planted when she saw that, in her hands, the sugar refinery was going to be a failure.

She sold out at a loss, and went on to Texas, where her husband had bought cheaply, some years before, a large tract of fertile black land in an almost unsettled part of the country. She had with her nine children, the youngest about two, the eldest about seventeen years old; Nannie and her three sons, Uncle Jimbilly, and two other Negroes, all in good health, full of hope and greatly desiring to live. Her husband's ghost persisted in her, she was bitterly outraged by his death almost as if he had willfully deserted her. She mourned for him at first with dry eyes, angrily. Twenty years later, seeing after a long absence the eldest son of her favorite daughter, who had died early, she recognized the very features and look of the husband of her youth, and she wept.

During the terrible second year in Texas, two of her younger sons, Harry and Robert, suddenly ran away. They chose good weather for it, in mid-May, and they were almost seven miles from home when a neighboring farmer saw them, wondered and asked questions, and ended by persuading them into his gig, and so brought them back.

Miss Sophia Jane went through the dreary ritual of discipline she thought appropriate to the occasion. She whipped them with her riding whip. Then she made them kneel down with her while she prayed for them, asking God to help them mend their ways and not be undutiful to their mother; her duty performed, she broke down and wept with her arms around them. They had endured their punishment stoically, because it would have been disgraceful to cry when a woman hit them, and besides, she did not hit very hard; they had knelt with her in a shamefaced gloom, because religious feeling was a female mystery which embarrassed them, but when they saw her tears they burst into loud bellows of repentance. They were only nine and eleven years old. She said in a voice of mourning, so despairing it frightened them: "Why did you run away from me? What do you think I brought you here for?" as if they were grown men who could realize how terrible the situation was. All the answer they could make, as they wept too, was that they had wanted to go back to Louisiana to eat sugar cane. They had been thinking about sugar cane all winter . . . Their mother was stunned. She had built a house large enough to shelter them all, of hand-sawed lumber dragged by ox-cart for forty miles, she had got the fields fenced in and the crops planted, she had, she believed, fed and clothed her children; and now she realized they were hungry. These two had worked like men; she felt their growing bones through their thin flesh, and remembered how mercilessly she had driven them, as she had driven herself, as she had driven the Negroes and the horses, because there was no choice in the matter. They must labor beyond their strength or perish. Sitting there with her arms around them, she felt her heart break in her breast. She had thought it was a silly phrase. It happened to her. It was not that she was incapable of feeling afterward, for in a way she was more emotional, more quick, but griefs never again lasted with her so long as they had before. This day was the beginning of her spoiling her children and being afraid of them. She said to them after a long dazed silence, when they began to grow restless under her arms: "We'll grow fine ribbon cane here. The soil is perfect for it. We'll have all the sugar we want. But we must be patient."

By the time her children began to marry, she was able to give them each a good strip of land and a little money, she was able to help them buy more land in places they preferred by selling her own, tract by tract, and she saw them all begin well, though not all of them ended so. They went about their own affairs, scattering out and seeming to lose all that sense of family unity so precious to the Grandmother. They bore with her infrequent visits and her advice and her tremendous rightness, and they were impatient of her tenderness. When Harry's wife died–she had never approved of Harry's wife, who was delicate and hopelessly inadequate at housekeeping, and who could not even bear children successfully, since she died when her third was born–the Grandmother took the children and began life again, with almost the same zest, and with more indulgence. She had just got them brought up to the point where she felt she could begin to work the faults out of them—faults inherited, she admitted fairly, from both sides of the house—when she died. It happened quite suddenly one afternoon in early October, after a day spent in helping the Mexican gardener of her third daughter-in-law to put the garden to rights. She was on a visit in far western Texas and enjoying it. The daughter-in-law was exasperated but apparently so docile, the Grandmother, who looked upon her as a child, did not notice her little moods at all. The son had long ago learned not to oppose his mother. She wore him down with patient, just, and reasonable argument. She was careful never to venture to command him in anything. He consoled his wife by saying that everything Mother was doing could be changed back after she was gone. As this change included moving a fifty-foot adobe wall, the wife was not much consoled. The Grandmother came into the house quite flushed and exhilarated, saying how well she felt in the bracing mountain air—and dropped dead over the doorsill.

THE LAST LEAF

The Last Leaf

OLD NANNIE sat hunched upon herself expecting her own death momentarily. The Grandmother had said to her at parting, with the easy prophecy of the aged, that this might be their last farewell on earth; they embraced and kissed each other on the cheeks, and once more promised to meet each other in heaven. Nannie was prepared to start her journey at once. The children gathered around her: "Aunt Nannie, never you mind! We love you!" She paid no attention; she did not care whether they loved her or not. Years afterward, Maria, the elder girl, thought with a pang, they had not really been so very nice to Aunt Nannie. They went on depending upon her as they always had, letting her assume more burdens and more, allowing her to work harder than she should have. The old woman grew silent, hunched over more deeply–she was thin and tall also, with a nobly modeled Negro face, worn to the bone and a thick fine sooty black, no mixed blood in Nannie–and her spine seemed suddenly to have given way. They could hear her groaning at night on her knees beside her bed, asking God to let her rest.

When a black family moved out of a little cabin across the narrow creek, the first cabin empty for years, Nannie went down to look at it. She came back and asked Mister Harry, "Whut you aim to do wid dat cabin?" Mister Harry said, "Nothing," he supposed; and Nannie asked for it. She wanted a house of her own, she said; in her whole life she never had a place of her very own. Mister Harry said, of course she could have it. But the whole family was surprised, a little wounded. "Lemme go there and pass my last days in peace, chil'ren," she said. They had the place scrubbed and whitewashed, shelves put in and the chimney cleaned, they fixed Nannie up with a good bed and a fairly good carpet and allowed her to take all sorts of odds and ends from the house. It was astonishing to discover that Nannie had always liked and hoped to own certain things, she had seemed so contented and wantless. She moved away, and as the children said afterwards to each other, it was almost funny and certainly very sweet to see how she tried not to be too happy the day she left, but they felt rather put upon, just the same.

Thereafter she sat in the serene idleness of making patchwork and braiding woolen rugs. Her grandchildren and her white family visited her, and all kinds of white persons who had never owned a soul related to Nannie, went to see her, to buy her rugs or leave little presents with her.

She had always worn black wool dresses, or black and white figured calico with starchy white aprons and a white ruffled mobcap, or a black taffety cap for Sundays. She had been finicking precise and neat in her ways, and she still was. But she was no more the faithful old servant Nannie, a freed slave: she was an aged Bantu woman of independent means, sitting on the steps, breathing the free air. She began wearing a blue bandanna wrapped around her head, and at the age of eighty-five she took to smoking a corncob pipe. The black iris of the deep, withdrawn old eyes turned a chocolate brown and seemed to spread over the whole surface of the eyeball. As her sight failed, the eyelids crinkled and drew in, so that her face was like an eyeless mask.

The children, brought up in an out-of-date sentimental way of thinking, had always complacently believed that Nannie was a real member of the family, perfectly happy with them, and this rebuke, so quietly and firmly administered, chastened them somewhat. The lesson sank in as the years went on and Nannie continued to sit on the doorstep of her cabin. They were growing up, times were changing, the old world was sliding from under their feet, they had not yet laid hold of the new one. They missed Nannie every day. As their fortunes went down, and they had very few servants, they needed her terribly. They realized how much the old woman had done for them, simply by seeing how, almost immediately after she went, everything slackened, lost tone, went off edge. Work did not accomplish itself as it once had. They had not learned how to work for themselves, they were all lazy and incapable of sustained effort or planning. They had not been taught and they had not yet educated themselves. Now and then Nannie would come back up the hill for a visit. She worked then almost as she had before, with a kind of satisfaction in proving to them that she had been almost indispensable. They would miss her more than ever when she went away. To show their gratitude, and their hope that she would come again, they would heap upon her baskets and bales of the precious rubbish she loved, and one of her great grandsons Skid or Hasty would push them away beside her on a wheelbarrow. She would again for a moment be the amiable, dependent, like-one-of-the-family old servant: "I know my chil'ren won't let me go away empty-handed."

Uncle Jimbilly still pottered around, mending harness, currying horses, patching fences, now and then setting out a few plants or loosening the earth around shrubs in the spring. He muttered perpetually to himself, his blue mouth always moving in an endless disjointed comment on things past and present, and even to come, no doubt, though there was nothing about him that suggested any connection with even the nearest future . . . Maria had not realized until after her grandmother's death that Uncle Jimbilly and Aunt Nannie were husband and wife . . . That marriage of convenience, in which they had been mated with truly royal policy, with an eye to the blood and family stability, had dissolved of itself between them when the reasons for its being had likewise dissolved . . . They took no notice whatever of each other's existence, they seemed to forget they had children together (each spoke of "my children"), they had stored up no common memories that either wished to keep. Aunt Nannie moved away into her own house without even a glance or thought for Uncle Jimbilly, and he did not seem to notice that she was gone . . . He slept in a little attic over the smoke-house, and ate in the kitchen at odd hours, and did as he pleased, lonely as a wandering spirit and almost as invisible . . . But one day he passed by the little house and saw Aunt Nannie sitting on her steps with her pipe. He sat down awhile, groaning a little as he bent himself into angles, and sunned himself like a weary old dog. He would have stayed on from that minute, but Nannie would not have him. "Whut you doin with all this big house to yoself?" he wanted to know. " 'Tain't no more than just enough fo' me," she told him pointedly; "I don' aim to pass my las' days waitin on no man," she added, "I've served my time, I've done my do, and dat's all." So Uncle Jimbilly crept back up the hill and into his smoke-house attic, and never went near her again . . .

✦

On summer evenings she sat by herself long after dark, smoking to keep away the mosquitoes, until she was ready to sleep. She said she wasn't afraid of anything: never had been, never expected to be. She had long ago got in the way of thinking that night was a blessing, it brought the time when she didn't have to work any more until tomorrow. Even after she stopped working for good and all, she still looked forward with longing to the night, as if all the accumulated fatigues of her life, lying now embedded in her bones, still begged for easement. But when night came, she remembered that she didn't have to get up in the morning until she was ready. So she would sit in the luxury of having at her disposal all of God's good time there was in this world.

When Mister Harry, in the old days, had stood out against her word in some petty dispute, she could always get the better of him by slapping her slatty old chest with the flat of her long hand and crying out: "Why, Mister Harry, you, ain't you shamed to talk lak dat to me? I nuhsed you at dis bosom!"

Harry knew this was not literally true. She had nursed three of his elder brothers; but he always said at once, "All right, Mammy, all right, for God's sake!"—precisely as he said it to his own mother, exploding in his natural irascibility as if he hoped to clear the air somewhat of the smothering matriarchal tyranny to which he had been delivered by the death of his father. Still he submitted, being of that latest generation of sons who acknowledged, however reluctantly, however bitterly, their mystical never to be forgiven debt to the womb that bore them, and the breast that suckled them.

THE GRAVE

The Grave

THE grandfather, dead for more than thirty years, had been twice disturbed in his long repose by the constancy and possessiveness of his widow. She removed his bones first to Louisiana and then to Texas as if she had set out to find her own burial place, knowing well she would never return to the places she had left. In Texas she set up a small cemetery in a corner of her first farm, and as the family connection grew, and oddments of relations came over from Kentucky to settle, it contained at last about twenty graves. After the grandmother's death, part of her land was to be sold for the benefit of certain of her children, and the cemetery happened to lie in the part set aside for sale. It was necessary to take up the bodies and bury them again in the family plot in the big new public cemetery, where the grandmother had been buried. At last her husband was to lie beside her for eternity, as she had planned.

The family cemetery had been a pleasant small neglected garden of tangled rose bushes and ragged cedar trees and cypress, the simple flat stones rising out of uncropped sweet-smelling wild grass. The graves were lying open and empty one burning day when Miranda and her brother Paul, who often went together to hunt rabbits and doves, propped their twenty-two Winchester rifles carefully against the rail fence, climbed over and explored among the graves. She was nine years old and he was twelve.

They peered into the pits all shaped alike with such purposeful accuracy, and looking at each other with pleased adventurous eyes, they said in solemn tones: "These were graves!" trying by words to shape a special, suitable emotion in their minds, but they felt nothing except an agreeable thrill of wonder: they were seeing a new sight, doing something they had not done before. In them both there was also a small disappointment at the entire commonplaceness of the actual spectacle. Even if it had once contained a coffin for years upon years, when the coffin was gone a grave was just a hole in the ground. Miranda leaped into the pit that had held her grandfather's bones. Scratching around aimlessly and pleasurably as any young animal, she scooped up a lump of earth and weighed it in her palm. It had a pleasantly sweet, corrupt smell, being mixed with cedar needles and small leaves, and as the crumbs fell apart, she saw a silver dove no larger than a hazel nut, with spread wings and a neat fan-shaped tail. The breast had a deep round hollow in it. Turning it up to the fierce sunlight, she saw that the inside of the hollow was cut in little whorls. She scrambled out, over the pile of loose earth that had fallen back into one end of the grave, calling to Paul that she had found something, he must guess what . . . His head appeared smiling over the rim of another grave. He waved a closed hand at her. "I've got something too!" They ran to compare treasures, making a game of it, so many guesses each, all wrong, and a final show-down with opened palms. Paul had found a thin wide gold ring carved with intricate flowers and leaves. Miranda was smitten at sight of the ring and wished to have it. Paul seemed more impressed by the dove. They made a trade, with some little bickering. After he had got the dove in his hand, Paul said, "Don't you know what this is? This is a screw head for a *coffin!* . . . I'll bet nobody else in the world has one like this!"

Miranda glanced at it without covetousness. She had the gold ring on her thumb; it fitted perfectly. "Maybe we ought to go now," she said, "maybe one of the niggers 'll see us and tell somebody." They knew the land had been sold, the cemetery was no longer theirs, and they felt like trespassers. They climbed back over the fence, slung their rifles loosely under their arms—they had been shooting at targets with various kinds of firearms since they were seven years old—and set out to look for the rabbits and doves or whatever small game might happen along. On these expeditions Miranda always followed at Paul's heels along the path, obeying instructions about handling her gun when going through fences; learning how to stand it up properly so it would not slip and fire unexpectedly; how to wait her time for a shot and not just bang away in the air without looking, spoiling shots for Paul, who really could hit things if given a chance. Now and then, in her excitement at seeing birds whizz up suddenly before her face, or a rabbit leap across her very toes, she lost her head, and almost without sighting she flung her rifle up and pulled the trigger. She hardly ever hit any sort of mark. She had no proper sense of hunting at all. Her brother would be often completely disgusted with her. "You don't care whether you get your bird or not," he said. "That's no way to hunt." Miranda could not understand his indignation. She had seen him smash his hat and yell with fury when he had missed his aim. "What I like about shooting," said Miranda, with exasperating inconsequence, "is pulling the trigger and hearing the noise."

"Then, by golly," said Paul, "whyn't you go back to the range and shoot at bulls-eyes?"

"I'd just as soon," said Miranda, "only like this, we walk around more."

"Well, you just stay behind and stop spoiling my shots," said Paul, who, when he made a kill, wanted to be certain he had made it. Miranda, who alone brought down a bird once in twenty rounds, always claimed as her own any game they got when they fired at the same moment. It was tiresome and unfair and her brother was sick of it.

"Now, the first dove we see, or the first rabbit, is mine,"

he told her. "And the next will be yours. Remember that and don't get smarty."

"What about snakes?" asked Miranda idly. "Can I have the first snake?"

Waving her thumb gently and watching her gold ring glitter, Miranda lost interest in shooting. She was wearing her summer roughing outfit: dark blue overalls, a light blue shirt, a hired-man's straw hat, and thick brown sandals. Her brother had the same outfit except his was a sober hickory-nut color. Ordinarily Miranda preferred her overalls to any other dress, though it was making rather a scandal in the countryside, for the year was 1903, and in the back country the law of female decorum had teeth in it. Her father had been criticized for letting his girls dress like boys and go careering around astride barebacked horses. Big sister Maria, the really independent and fearless one, in spite of her rather affected ways, rode at a dead run with only a rope knotted around her horse's nose. It was said the motherless family was running down, with the Grandmother no longer there to hold it together. It was known that she had discriminated against her son Harry in her will, and that he was in straits about money. Some of his old neighbors reflected with vicious satisfaction that now he would probably not be so stiffnecked, nor have any more high-stepping horses either. Miranda knew this, though she could not say how. She had met along the road old women of the kind who smoked corn-cob pipes, who had treated her grandmother with most sincere respect. They slanted their gummy old eyes side-ways at the granddaughter and said, "Ain't you ashamed of yoself, Missy? It's aginst the Scriptures to dress like that. Whut yo Pappy thinkin about?" Miranda, with her powerful social sense, which was like a fine set of antennae radiating from every pore of her skin, would feel ashamed because she knew well it was rude and ill-bred to shock anybody, even bad-tempered old crones, though she had faith in her father's judgment and was perfectly comfortable in the clothes. Her father had said, "They're just what you need, and they'll save your dresses for school . . ." This sounded quite simple and natural to her. She had been brought up in rigorous economy. Wastefulness was vulgar. It was also a sin. These were truths; she had heard them repeated many times and never once disputed.

Now the ring, shining with the serene purity of fine gold on her rather grubby thumb, turned her feelings against her overalls and sockless feet, toes sticking through the thick brown leather straps. She wanted to go back to the farmhouse, take a good cold bath, dust herself with plenty of Maria's violet talcum powder—provided Maria was not present to object, of course—put on the thinnest, most becoming dress she owned, with a big sash, and sit in a wicker chair under the trees . . . These things were not all she wanted, of course; she had vague stirrings of desire for luxury and a grand way of living which could not take precise form in her imagination but were founded on family legend of past wealth and leisure. These immediate comforts were what she could have, and she wanted them at once. She lagged rather far behind Paul, and once she thought of just turning back without a word and going home. She stopped, thinking that Paul would never do that to her, and so she would have to tell him. When a rabbit leaped, she let Paul have it without dispute. He killed it with one shot.

When she came up with him, he was already kneeling, examining the wound, the rabbit trailing from his hands. "Right through the head," he said complacently, as if he had aimed for it. He took out his sharp, competent bowie knife and started to skin the body. He did it very cleanly and quickly. Uncle Jimbilly knew how to prepare the skins so that Miranda always had fur coats for her dolls, for though she never cared much for her dolls she liked seeing them in fur coats. The children knelt facing each other over the dead animal. Miranda watched admiringly while her brother stripped the skin away as if he were taking off a glove. The flayed flesh emerged dark scarlet, sleek, firm; Miranda with thumb and finger felt the long fine muscles with the silvery flat strips binding them to the joints. Brother lifted the oddly bloated belly. "Look," he said, in a low amazed voice. "It was going to have young ones."

Very carefully he slit the thin flesh from the center ribs

to the flanks, and a scarlet bag appeared. He slit again and pulled the bag open, and there lay a bundle of tiny rabbits, each wrapped in a thin scarlet veil. The brother pulled these off and there they were, dark gray, their sleek wet down lying in minute even ripples, like a baby's head just washed, their unbelievably small delicate ears folded close, their little blind faces almost featureless.

Miranda said, "Oh, I want to *see*," under her breath. She looked and looked–excited but not frightened, for she was accustomed to the sight of animals killed in hunting–filled with pity and astonishment and a kind of shocked delight in the wonderful little creatures for their own sakes, they were so pretty. She touched one of them ever so carefully, "Ah, there's blood running over them," she said and began to tremble without knowing why. Yet she wanted most deeply to see and to know. Having seen, she felt at once as if she had known all along. The very memory of her former ignorance faded, she had always known just this. No one had ever told her anything outright, she had been rather unobservant of the animal life around her because she was so accustomed to animals. They seemed simply disorderly and unaccountably rude in their habits, but altogether natural and not very interesting. Her brother had spoken as if he had known about everything all along. He may have seen all this before. He had never said a word to her, but she knew now a part at least of what he knew. She understood a little of the secret, formless intuitions in her own mind and body, which had been clearing up, taking form, so gradually and so steadily she had not realized that she was learning what she had to know. Paul said cautiously, as if he were talking about something forbidden: "They were just about ready to be born." His voice dropped on the last word. "I know," said Miranda, "like kittens. I know, like babies." She was quietly and terribly agitated, standing again with her rifle under her arm, looking down at the bloody heap. "I don't want the skin," she said, "I won't have it." Paul buried the young rabbits again in their mother's body, wrapped the skin around her, carried her to a clump of sage bushes, and hid her away. He came out again at once and said to Miranda, with an eager friendliness, a confidential tone quite unusual in him, as if he were taking her into an important secret on equal terms: "Listen now. Now you listen to me, and don't ever forget. Don't you ever tell a living soul that you saw this. Don't tell a soul. Don't tell Dad because I'll get into trouble. He'll say I'm leading you into things you ought not to do. He's always saying that. So now don't you go and forget and blab out sometime the way you're always doing . . . Now, that's a secret. Don't you tell."

Miranda never told, she did not even wish to tell anybody. She thought about the whole worrisome affair with confused unhappiness for a few days. Then it sank quietly into her mind and was heaped over by accumulated thousands of impressions, for nearly twenty years. One day she was picking her path among the puddles and crushed refuse of a market street in a strange city of a strange country, when without warning, plain and clear in its true colors as if she looked through a frame upon a scene that had not stirred nor changed since the moment it happened, the episode of that far-off day leaped from its burial place before her mind's eye. She was so reasonlessly horrified she halted suddenly staring, the scene before her eyes dimmed by the vision back of them. An Indian vendor had held up before her a tray of dyed sugar sweets, in the shapes of all kinds of small creatures: birds, baby chicks, baby rabbits, lambs, baby pigs. They were in gay colors and smelled of vanilla, maybe. . . . It was a very hot day and the smell in the market, with its piles of raw flesh and wilting flowers, was like the mingled sweetness and corruption she had smelled that other day in the empty cemetery at home: the day she had remembered always until now vaguely as the time she and her brother had found treasure in the opened graves. Instantly upon this thought the dreadful vision faded, and she saw clearly her brother, whose childhood face she had forgotten, standing again in the blazing sunshine, again twelve years old, a pleased sober smile in his eyes, turning the silver dove over and over in his hands.

THE DOWNWARD PATH TO WISDOM

The Downward Path to Wisdom

IN the square bedroom with the big window Mama and Papa were lolling back on their pillows handing each other things from the wide black tray on the small table with crossed legs. They were smiling and they smiled even more when the little boy, with the feeling of sleep still in his skin and hair, came in and walked up to the bed. Leaning against it, his bare toes wriggling in the white fur rug, he went on eating peanuts which he took from his pajama pocket. He was four years old.

"Here's my baby," said Mama. "Lift him up, will you?"

He went limp as a rag for Papa to take him under the arms and swing him up over a broad, tough chest. He sank between his parents like a bear cub in a warm litter, and lay there comfortably. He took another peanut between his teeth, cracked the shell, picked out the nut whole and ate it.

"Running around without his slippers again," said Mama. "His feet are like icicles."

"He crunches like a horse," said Papa. "Eating peanuts before breakfast will ruin his stomach. Where did he get them?"

"You brought them yesterday," said Mama, with exact memory, "in a grisly little cellophane sack. I have asked you dozens of times not to bring him things to eat. Put him out, will you? He's spilling shells all over me."

Almost at once the little boy found himself on the floor again. He moved around to Mama's side of the bed and leaned confidingly near her and began another peanut. As he chewed he gazed solemnly in her eyes.

"Bright-looking specimen, isn't he?" asked Papa, stretching his long legs and reaching for his bathrobe. "I suppose you'll say it's my fault he's dumb as an ox."

"He's my little baby, my only baby," said Mama richly, hugging him, "and he's a dear lamb." His neck and shoulders were quite boneless in her firm embrace. He stopped chewing long enough to receive a kiss on his crumby chin. "He's sweet as clover," said Mama. The baby went on chewing.

"Look at him staring like an owl," said Papa.

Mama said, "He's an angel and I'll never get used to having him."

"We'd be better off if we never *had* had him," said Papa. He was walking about the room and his back was turned when he said that. There was silence for a moment. The little boy stopped eating, and stared deeply at his Mama. She was looking at the back of Papa's head, and her eyes were almost black. "You're going to say that just once too often," she told him in a low voice. "I hate you when you say that."

Papa said, "You spoil him to death. You never correct him

for anything. And you don't take care of him. You let him run around eating peanuts before breakfast."

"You gave him the peanuts, remember that," said Mama. She sat up and hugged her only baby once more. He nuzzled softly in the pit of her arm. "Run along, my darling," she told him in her gentlest voice, smiling at him straight in the eyes. "Run along," she said, her arms falling away from him. "Get your breakfast."

The little boy had to pass his father on the way to the door. He shrank into himself when he saw the big hand raised above him. "Yes, get out of here and stay out," said Papa, giving him a little shove toward the door. It was not a hard shove, but it hurt the little boy. He slunk out, and trotted down the hall trying not to look back. He was afraid something was coming after him, he could not imagine what. Something hurt him all over, he did not know why.

He did not want his breakfast; he would not have it. He sat and stirred it round in the yellow bowl, letting it stream off the spoon and spill on the table, on his front, on the chair. He liked seeing it spill. It was hateful stuff, but it looked funny running in white rivulets down his pajamas.

"Now look what you're doing, dirty boy," said Marjory. "You dirty little old boy."

The little boy opened his mouth to speak for the first time. "You're dirty yourself," he told her.

"That's right," said Marjory, leaning over him and speaking so her voice would not carry. "That's right, just like your papa. Mean," she whispered, "mean."

The little boy took up his yellow bowl full of cream and oatmeal and sugar with both hands and brought it down with a crash on the table. It burst and some of the wreck lay in chunks and some of it ran all over everything. He felt better.

"You see?" said Marjory, dragging him out of the chair and scrubbing him with a napkin. She scrubbed him as roughly as she dared until he cried out. "That's just what I said. That's exactly it." Through his tears he saw her face terribly near, red and frowning under a stiff white band, looking like the face of somebody who came at night and stood over him and scolded him when he could not move or get away. "Just like your papa, *mean*."

The little boy went out into the garden and sat on a green bench dangling his legs. He was clean. His hair was wet and his blue woolly pull-over made his nose itch. His face felt stiff from the soap. He saw Marjory going past a window with the black tray. The curtains were still closed at the window he knew opened into Mama's room. Papa's room. Mommanpoppasroom, the word was pleasant, it made a mumbling snapping noise between his lips; it ran in his mind while his eyes wandered about looking for something to do, something to play with.

Mommanpoppas' voices kept attracting his attention.

Mama was being cross with Papa again. He could tell by the sound. That was what Marjory always said when their voices rose and fell and shot up to a point and crashed and rolled like the two tomcats who fought at night. Papa was being cross, too, much crosser than Mama this time. He grew cold and disturbed and sat very still, wanting to go to the bathroom, but it was just next to Mommanpoppasroom; he didn't dare think of it. As the voices grew louder he could hardly hear them any more, he wanted so badly to go to the bathroom. The kitchen door opened suddenly and Marjory ran out, making the motion with her hand that meant he was to come to her. He didn't move. She came to him, her face still red and frowning, but she was not angry; she was scared just as he was. She said, "Come on, honey, we've got to go to your gran'ma's again." She took his hand and pulled him. "Come on quick, your gran'ma is waiting for you." He slid off the bench. His mother's voice rose in a terrible scream, screaming something he could not understand, but she was furious; he had seen her clenching her fists and stamping in one spot, screaming with her eyes shut; he knew how she looked. She was screaming in a tantrum, just as he remembered having heard himself. He stood still, doubled over, and all his body seemed to dissolve, sickly, from the pit of his stomach.

"Oh, my God," said Marjory. "Oh, my God. Now look at you. Oh, my God. I can't stop to clean you up."

He did not know how he got to his grandma's house, but he was there at last, wet and soiled, being handled with disgust in the big bathtub. His grandma was there in long black skirts saying, "Maybe he's sick; maybe we should send for the doctor."

"I don't think so, m'am," said Marjory. "He hasn't et anything; he's just scared."

The little boy couldn't raise his eyes, he was so heavy with shame. "Take this note to his mother," said Grandma.

She sat in a wide chair and ran her hands over his head, combing his hair with her fingers; she lifted his chin and kissed him. "Poor little fellow," she said. "Never you mind. You always have a good time at your grandma's, don't you? You're going to have a nice little visit, just like the last time."

The little boy leaned against the stiff, dry-smelling clothes and felt horribly grieved about something. He began to whimper and said, "I'm hungry. I want something to eat." This reminded him. He began to bellow at the top of his voice; he threw himself upon the carpet and rubbed his nose in a dusty woolly bouquet of roses. "I want my peanuts," he howled. "Somebody took my peanuts."

His grandma knelt beside him and gathered him up so tightly he could hardly move. She called in a calm voice above his howls to Old Janet in the doorway, "Bring me some bread and butter with strawberry jam."

"I want peanuts," yelled the little boy desperately.

"No, you don't, darling," said his grandma. "You don't want horrid old peanuts to make you sick. You're going to have some of grandma's nice fresh bread with good strawberries on it. That's what you're going to have." He sat afterward very quietly and ate and ate. His grandma sat near him and Old Janet stood by, near a tray with a loaf and a glass bowl of jam upon the table at the window. Outside there was a trellis with tube-shaped red flowers clinging all over it, and brown bees singing.

"I hardly know what to do," said Grandma, "it's very . . ."

"Yes, m'am," said Old Janet, "it certainly is . . ."

Grandma said, "I can't possibly see the end of it. It's a terrible . . ."

"It certainly is bad," said Old Janet, "all this upset all the time and him such a baby."

Their voices ran on soothingly. The little boy ate and forgot to listen. He did not know these women, except by name. He could not understand what they were talking about; their hands and their clothes and their voices were dry and far away; they examined him with crinkled eyes without any expression that he could see. He sat there waiting for whatever they would do next with him. He hoped they would let him go out and play in the yard. The room was full of flowers and dark red curtains and big soft chairs, and the windows were open, but it was still dark in there somehow; dark, and a place he did not know, or trust.

"Now drink your milk," said Old Janet, holding out a silver cup.

"I don't want any milk," he said, turning his head away.

"Very well, Janet, he doesn't have to drink it," said Grandma quickly. "Now run out in the garden and play, darling. Janet, get his hoop."

A big strange man came home in the evenings who treated the little boy very confusingly. "Say 'please,' and 'thank you,' young man," he would roar, terrifyingly, when he gave any smallest object to the little boy. "Well, fellow, are you ready for a fight?" he would say, again, doubling up huge, hairy fists and making passes at him. "Come on now, you must learn to box." After the first few times this was fun.

"Don't teach him to be rough," said Grandma. "Time enough for all that."

"Now, Mother, we don't want him to be a sissy," said the big man. "He's got to toughen up early. Come on now, fellow, put up your mitts." The little boy liked this new word for hands. He learned to throw himself upon the strange big man, whose name was Uncle David, and hit him on the chest as hard as he could; the big man would laugh and hit him back with his huge, loose fists. Sometimes, but not often, Uncle David came home in the middle of the day. The little boy missed him on the other days, and would hang on the gate looking down the street for him. One evening he brought a large square package under his arm.

"Come over here, fellow, and see what I've got," he said, pulling off quantities of green paper and string from the box which was full of flat, folded colors. He put something in the little boy's hand. It was limp and silky and bright green with a tube on the end. "Thank you," said the little boy nicely, but not knowing what to do with it.

"Balloons," said Uncle David in triumph. "Now just put your mouth here and blow hard." The little boy blew hard and the green thing began to grow round and thin and silvery.

"Good for your chest," said Uncle David. "Blow some more." The little boy went on blowing and the balloon swelled steadily.

"Stop," said Uncle David, "that's enough." He twisted the tube to keep the air in. "That's the way," he said. "Now I'll blow one, and you blow one, and let's see who can blow up a big balloon the fastest."

They blew and blew, especially Uncle David. He puffed and panted and blew with all his might, but the little boy won. His balloon was perfectly round before Uncle David could even get started. The little boy was so proud he began to dance and shout, "I beat, I beat," and blew in his balloon again. It burst in his face and frightened him so he felt sick.

"Ha ha, ho ho ho," whooped Uncle David. "That's the boy. I bet I can't do that. Now let's see." He blew until the beautiful bubble grew and wavered and burst into thin air, and there was only a small colored rag in his hand. This was a fine game. They went on with it until Grandma came in and said, "Time for supper now. No, you can't blow balloons at the table. Tomorrow maybe." And it was all over.

The next day, instead of being given balloons, he was hustled out of bed early, bathed in warm soapy water and given a big breakfast of soft-boiled eggs with toast and jam and milk. His grandma came in to kiss him good morning. "And I hope you'll be a good boy and obey your teacher," she told him.

"What's teacher?" asked the little boy.

"Teacher is at school," said Grandma. "She'll tell you all sorts of things and you must do as she says."

Mama and Papa had talked a great deal about School, and how they must send him there. They had told him it was a fine place with all kinds of toys and other children to play with. He felt he knew about School. "I didn't know it was time, Grandma," he said. "Is it today?"

"It's this very minute," said Grandma. "I told you a week ago."

Old Janet came in with her bonnet on. It was a prickly looking bundle held with a black rubber band under her back hair. "Come on," she said. "This is my busy day." She wore a dead cat slung around her neck, its sharp ears bent over under her baggy chin.

The little boy was excited and wanted to run ahead. "Hold to my hand like I told you," said Old Janet. "Don't go running off like that and get yourself killed."

"I'm going to get killed, I'm going to get killed," sang the little boy, making a tune of his own.

"Don't say that, you give me the creeps," said Old Janet. "Hold to my hand now." She bent over and looked at him, not at his face but at something on his clothes. His eyes followed hers.

"I declare," said Old Janet, "I did forget. I was going to sew it up. I might have known. I *told* your grandma it would be that way from now on."

"What?" asked the little boy.

"Just look at yourself," said Old Janet crossly. He looked at himself. There was a little end of him showing through the slit in his short blue flannel trousers. The trousers came halfway to his knees above, and his socks came halfway to his knees below, and all winter long his knees were cold. He remembered now how cold his knees were in cold weather. And how sometimes he would have to put the part of him that came through the slit back again, because he was cold there too. He saw at once what was wrong, and tried to arrange himself, but his mittens got in the way. Janet said, "Stop that, you bad boy," and with a firm thumb she set him in order, at the same time reaching under his belt to pull down and fold his knit undershirt over his front.

"There now," she said, "try not to disgrace yourself today." He felt guilty and red all over, because he had something that showed when he was dressed that was not supposed to show then. The different women who bathed him always wrapped him quickly in towels and hurried him into his clothes, because they saw something about him he could not see for himself. They hurried him so he never had a chance to see whatever it was they saw, and though he looked at himself when his clothes were off, he could not find out what was wrong with him. Outside, in his clothes, he knew he looked like everybody else, but inside his clothes there was something bad the matter with him. It worried him and confused him and he wondered about it. The only people who never seemed to notice there was something wrong with him were Mommanpoppa. They never called him a bad boy, and all summer long they had taken all his clothes off and let him run in the sand beside a big ocean.

"Look at him, isn't he a love?" Mama would say and Papa would look, and say, "He's got a back like a prize fighter." Uncle David was a prize fighter when he doubled up his mitts and said, "Come on, fellow."

Old Janet held him firmly and took long steps under her big rustling skirts. He did not like Old Janet's smell. It made him a little quivery in the stomach; it was just like wet chicken feathers.

School was easy. Teacher was a square-shaped woman with square short hair and short skirts. She got in the way sometimes, but not often. The people around him were his size; he didn't have always to be stretching his neck up to faces bent over him, and he could sit on the chairs without having to climb. All the children had names, like Frances and Evelyn and Agatha and Edward and Martin, and his own name was Stephen. He was not Mama's "Baby," nor Papa's "Old Man"; he was not Uncle David's "Fellow" or Grandma's "Darling," or even Old Janet's "Bad Boy." He was Stephen. He was learning to read, and to sing a tune to some strange-looking letters or marks written in chalk on a blackboard. You talked one kind of lettering, and you sang another. All the children talked and sang in turn, and then all together. Stephen thought it a fine game. He felt awake and happy. They had soft clay and paper and wires and squares of colors in tin boxes to play with, colored blocks to build houses with. Afterward they all danced in a big ring, and then they danced in pairs, boys with girls. Stephen danced with Frances, and Frances kept saying, "Now you just follow me." She was a little taller than he was, and her hair stood up in short, shiny curls, the color of an ash tray on Papa's desk. She would say, "You can't dance." "I can dance too," said Stephen, jumping around holding her hands, "I can, too, dance." He was certain of it. "*You* can't dance," he told Frances, "you can't dance at all."

Then they had to change partners, and when they came round again, Frances said, "I don't *like* the way you dance." This was different. He felt uneasy about it. He didn't jump quite so high when the phonograph record started going dumdiddy dumdiddy again. "Go ahead, Stephen, you're doing fine," said Teacher, waving her hands together very fast. The dance ended, and they all played "relaxing" for five minutes. They relaxed by swinging their arms back and forth, then rolling their heads round and round. When Old Janet came for him he didn't want to go home. At lunch his grandma told him twice to keep his face out of his plate. "Is that what they teach you at school?" she asked. Uncle David was at home. "Here you are, fellow," he said and gave Stephen two balloons. "Thank you," said Stephen. He put the balloons in his pocket and forgot about them. "I told you that boy could learn something," said Uncle David to Grandma. "Hear him say 'thank you'?"

In the afternoon at school Teacher handed out big wads of clay and told the children to make something out of it. Anything they liked. Stephen decided to make a cat, like Mama's Meeow at home. He did not like Meeow, but he thought it would be easy to make a cat. He could not get the clay to work at all. It simply fell into one lump after another. So he stopped, wiped his hands on his pull-over, remembered his balloons and began blowing one.

"Look at Stephen's horse," said Frances. "Just look at it."

"It's not a horse, it's a cat," said Stephen. The other children gathered around. "It looks like a horse, a little," said Martin.

"It is a cat," said Stephen, stamping his foot, feeling his face turning hot. The other children all laughed and exclaimed over Stephen's cat that looked like a horse. Teacher came down among them. She sat usually at the top of the room before a big table covered with papers and playthings. She picked up Stephen's lump of clay and turned it round and examined it with her kind eyes. "Now, children," she said, "everybody has the right to make anything the way he pleases. If Stephen says this is a cat, it *is* a cat. Maybe you were thinking about a horse, Stephen?"

"It's a *cat*," said Stephen. He was aching all over. He knew then he should have said at first, "Yes, it's a horse." Then they would have let him alone. They would never have known he was trying to make a cat. "It's Meeow," he said in a trembling voice, "but I forgot how she looks."

His balloon was perfectly flat. He started blowing it up again, trying not to cry. Then it was time to go home, and Old Janet came looking for him. While Teacher was talking to other grown-up people who came to take other children home, Frances said, "Give me your balloon; I haven't got a balloon." Stephen handed it to her. He was happy to give it. He reached in his pocket and took out the other. Happily, he gave her that one too. Frances took it, then handed it back. "Now you blow up one and I'll blow up the other, and let's have a race," she said. When their balloons were only half filled Old Janet took Stephen by the arm and said, "Come on here, this is my busy day."

Frances ran after them, calling, "Stephen, you give me back my balloon," and snatched it away. Stephen did not know whether he was surprised to find himself going away with Frances' balloon, or whether he was surprised to see her snatching it as if it really belonged to her. He was badly mixed up in his mind, and Old Janet was hauling him along. One thing he knew, he liked Frances, he was going to see her again tomorrow, and he was going to bring her more balloons.

That evening Stephen boxed awhile with his uncle David, and Uncle David gave him a beautiful orange. "Eat that," he said, "it's good for your health."

"Uncle David, may I have some more balloons?" asked Stephen.

"Well, what do you say first?" asked Uncle David, reaching for the box on the top bookshelf.

"Please," said Stephen.

"That's the word," said Uncle David. He brought out two balloons, a red and a yellow one. Stephen noticed for the first time they had letters on them, very small letters that grew taller and wider as the balloon grew rounder. "Now that's all, fellow," said Uncle David. "Don't ask for any more because that's all." He put the box back on the bookshelf, but not before Stephen had seen that the box was almost full of balloons. He didn't say a word, but went on blowing, and Uncle David blew also. Stephen thought it was the nicest game he had ever known.

He had only one left, the next day, but he took it to school and gave it to Frances. "There are a lot," he said, feeling very proud and warm; "I'll bring you a lot of them."

Frances blew it up until it made a beautiful bubble, and said, "Look, I want to show you something." She took a sharp-pointed stick they used in working the clay; she poked the balloon, and it exploded. "Look at that," she said.

"That's nothing," said Stephen, "I'll bring you some more."

After school, before Uncle David came home, while Grandma was resting, when Old Janet had given him his milk and told him to run away and not bother her, Stephen dragged a chair to the bookshelf, stood upon it and reached into the box. He did not take three or four as he believed he intended; once his hands were upon them he seized what they could hold and jumped off the chair, hugging them to him. He stuffed them into his reefer pocket where they folded down and hardly made a lump.

He gave them all to Frances. There were so many, Frances

gave most of them away to the other children. Stephen, flushed with his new joy, the lavish pleasure of giving presents, found almost at once still another happiness. Suddenly he was popular among the children; they invited him specially to join whatever games were up; they fell in at once with his own notions for play, and asked him what he would like to do next. They had festivals of blowing up the beautiful globes, fuller and rounder and thinner, changing as they went from deep color to lighter, paler tones, growing glassy thin, bubbly thin, then bursting with a thrilling loud noise like a toy pistol.

For the first time in his life Stephen had almost too much of something he wanted, and his head was so turned he forgot how this fullness came about, and no longer thought of it as a secret. The next day was Saturday, and Frances came to visit him with her nurse. The nurse and Old Janet sat in Old Janet's room drinking coffee and gossiping, and the children sat on the side porch blowing balloons. Stephen chose an apple-colored one and Frances a pale green one. Between them on the bench lay a tumbled heap of delights still to come.

"I once had a silver balloon," said Frances, "a beyootiful silver one, not round like these; it was a long one. But these are even nicer, I think," she added quickly, for she did want to be polite.

"When you get through with that one," said Stephen,

gazing at her with the pure bliss of giving added to loving, "you can blow up a blue one and then a pink one and a yellow one and a purple one" He pushed the heap of limp objects toward her. Her clear-looking eyes, with fine little rays of brown in them like the spokes of a wheel, were full of approval for Stephen. "I wouldn't want to be greedy, though, and blow up all your balloons."

"There'll be plenty more left," said Stephen, and his heart rose under his thin ribs. He felt his ribs with his fingers and discovered with some surprise that they stopped somewhere in front, while Frances sat blowing balloons rather halfheartedly. The truth was, she was tired of balloons. After you blow six or seven your chest gets hollow and your lips feel puckery. She had been blowing balloons steadily for three days now. She had begun to hope they were giving out. "There's boxes and boxes more of them, Frances," said Stephen happily. "Millions more. I guess they'd last and last if we didn't blow too many every day."

Frances said somewhat timidly, "I tell you what. Let's rest awhile and fix some liquish water. Do you like liquish?"

"Yes, I do," said Stephen, "but I haven't got any."

"Couldn't we buy some?" asked Frances. "It's only a cent a stick, the nice rubbery, twisty kind. We can put it in a bottle with some water, and shake it and shake it, and it makes foam on top like soda pop and we can drink it. I'm kind of thirsty," she said in a small, weak voice. "Blowing balloons all the time makes you thirsty, I think."

Stephen, in silence, realized a dreadful truth and a numb feeling crept over him. He did not have a cent to buy licorice for Frances and she was tired of his balloons. This was the first real dismay of his whole life, and he aged at least a year in the next minute, huddled, with his deep, serious blue eyes focused down his nose in intense speculation. What could he do to please Frances that would not cost money? Only yesterday Uncle David had given him a nickel, and he had thrown it away on gumdrops. He regretted that nickel so bitterly his neck and forehead were damp. He was thirsty too.

"I tell you what," he said, brightening with a splendid idea, lamely trailing off on second thought, "I know something we can do, I'll–I . . ."

"I *am* thirsty," said Frances with gentle persistence. "I think I'm so thirsty maybe I'll have to go home." She did not leave the bench, though, but sat, turning her grieved mouth toward Stephen.

Stephen quivered with the terrors of the adventure before him, but he said boldly, "I'll make some lemonade. I'll get sugar and lemon and some ice and we'll have lemonade."

"Oh, I love lemonade," cried Frances. "I'd rather have lemonade than liquish."

"You stay right here," said Stephen, "and I'll get everything."

He ran around the house, and under Old Janet's window he heard the dry, chattering voices of the two old women whom he must outwit. He sneaked on tiptoe to the pantry, took a lemon lying there by itself, a handful of lump sugar and a china teapot, smooth, round, with flowers and leaves all over it. These he left on the kitchen table while he broke a piece of ice with a sharp metal pick he had been forbidden to touch. He put the ice in the pot, cut the lemon and squeezed it as well as he could—a lemon was tougher and more slippery than he had thought—and mixed sugar and water. He decided there was not enough sugar so he sneaked back and took another handful. He was back on the porch in an astonishingly short time, his face tight, his knees trembling, carrying iced lemonade to thirsty Frances with both his devoted hands.

A pace distant from her he stopped, literally stabbed through with a thought. Here he stood in broad daylight carrying a teapot with lemonade in it, and his grandma or Old Janet might walk through the door at any moment.

"Come on, Frances," he whispered loudly. "Let's go round to the back behind the rose bushes where it's shady." Frances leaped up and ran like a deer beside him, her face wise with knowledge of why they ran; Stephen ran stiffly, cherishing his teapot with clenched hands.

It was shady behind the rose bushes, and much safer. They sat side by side on the dampish ground, legs doubled under, drinking in turn from the slender spout. Stephen took his just share in large, cool, delicious swallows. When Frances drank she set her round pink mouth daintily to the spout and her throat beat steadily as a heart. Stephen was thinking he had really done something pretty nice for Frances. He did not know where his own happiness was; it was mixed with the sweet-sour taste in his mouth and a cool feeling in his bosom because Frances was there drinking his lemonade which he had got for her with great danger.

Frances said, "My, what big swallows you take," when his turn came next.

"No bigger than yours," he told her downrightly. "You take awfully big swallows."

"Well," said Frances, turning this criticism into an argument for her rightness about things, "that's the way to drink lemonade anyway." She peered into the teapot. There was quite a lot of lemonade left and she was beginning to feel she had enough. "Let's make up a game and see who can take the biggest swallows."

This was such a wonderful notion they grew reckless, tipping the spout into their opened mouths above their heads until lemonade welled up and ran over their chins in rills down their fronts. When they tired of this there was still lemonade left in the pot. They played first at giving the rosebush a drink and ended by baptizing it. "Name father son holygoat," shouted Stephen, pouring. At this sound Old Janet's face appeared over the low hedge, with the tan, disgusted-looking face of Frances' nurse hanging over her shoulder.

"Well, just as I thought," said Old Janet. "Just as I expected." The bag under her chin waggled.

"We were thirsty," he said; "we were awfully thirsty." Frances said nothing, but she gazed steadily at the toes of her shoes.

"Give me that teapot," said Old Janet, taking it with a rude snatch. "Just because you're thirsty is no reason," said Old Janet. "You can ask for things. You don't have to steal."

"We didn't steal," cried Frances suddenly. "We didn't. We didn't!"

"That's enough from you, missy," said her nurse. "Come straight out of there. You have nothing to do with this."

"Oh, I don't know," said Old Janet with a hard stare at Frances' nurse. "*He* never did such a thing before, by himself."

"Come on," said the nurse to Frances, "this is no place for you." She held Frances by the wrist and started walking away so fast Frances had to run to keep up. "Nobody can call *us* thieves and get away with it."

"You don't have to steal, even if others do," said Old Janet to Stephen, in a high carrying voice. "If you so much as pick up a lemon in somebody else's house you're a little thief." She lowered her voice then and said, "Now I'm going to tell your grandma and you'll see what you get."

"He went in the icebox and left it open," Janet told Grandma, "and he got into the lump sugar and spilt it all over the floor. Lumps everywhere underfoot. He dribbled water all over the clean kitchen floor, and he baptized the rose bush, blaspheming. And he took your Spode teapot."

"I didn't either," said Stephen loudly, trying to free his hand from Old Janet's big hard fist.

"Don't tell fibs," said Old Janet; "that's the last straw."

"Oh, dear," said Grandma. "He's not a baby any more." She shut the book she was reading and pulled the wet front of his pull-over toward her. "What's this sticky stuff on him?" she asked and straightened her glasses.

"Lemonade," said Old Janet. "He took the last lemon."

They were in the big dark room with the red curtains. Uncle David walked in from the room with the bookcases, holding a box in his uplifted hand. "Look here," he said to Stephen. "What's become of all my balloons?"

Stephen knew well that Uncle David was not really asking a question.

Stephen, sitting on a footstool at his grandma's knee, felt sleepy. He leaned heavily and wished he could put his head on her lap, but he might go to sleep, and it would be wrong to go to sleep while Uncle David was still talking. Uncle

David walked about the room with his hands in his pockets, talking to Grandma. Now and then he would walk over to a lamp and, leaning, peer into the top of the shade, winking in the light, as if he expected to find something there.

"It's simply in the blood, I told her," said Uncle David. "I told her she would simply have to come and get him, and keep him. She asked me if I meant to call him a thief and I said if she could think of a more exact word I'd be glad to hear it."

"You shouldn't have said that," commented Grandma calmly.

"Why not? She might as well know the facts. . . . I suppose he can't help it," said Uncle David, stopping now in front of Stephen and dropping his chin into his collar, "I shouldn't expect too much of him, but you can't begin too early—"

"The trouble is," said Grandma, and while she spoke she took Stephen by the chin and held it up so that he had to meet her eye; she talked steadily in a mournful tone, but Stephen could not understand. She ended, "It's not just about the balloons, of course."

"It *is* about the balloons," said Uncle David angrily, "because balloons now mean something worse later. But what can you expect? His father—well, it's in the blood. He—"

"That's your sister's husband you're talking about," said

Grandma, "and there is no use making things worse. Besides, you don't really *know*."

"I *do* know," said Uncle David. And he talked again very fast, walking up and down. Stephen tried to understand, but the sounds were strange and floating just over his head. They were talking about his father, and they did not like him. Uncle David came over and stood above Stephen and Grandma. He hunched over them with a frowning face, a long, crooked shadow from him falling across them to the wall. To Stephen he looked like his father, and he shrank against his grandma's skirts.

"The question is, what to do with him now?" asked Uncle David. "If we keep him here, he'd just be a—I won't be bothered with him. Why can't they take care of their own child? That house is crazy. Too far gone already, I'm afraid. No training. No example."

"You're right, they must take him and keep him," said Grandma. She ran her hands over Stephen's head; tenderly she pinched the nape of his neck between thumb and forefinger. "You're your Grandma's darling," she told him, "and you've had a nice long visit, and now you're going home. Mama is coming for you in a few minutes. Won't that be nice? '

"I want my mama," said Stephen, whimpering, for his grandma's face frightened him. There was something wrong with her smile.

Uncle David sat down. "Come over here, fellow," he said, wagging a forefinger at Stephen. Stephen went over slowly, and Uncle David drew him between his wide knees in their loose, rough clothes. "You ought to be ashamed of yourself," he said, "stealing Uncle David's balloons when he had already given you so many."

"It wasn't that," said Grandma quickly. "Don't say that. It will make an impression—"

"I hope it does," said Uncle David in a louder voice; "I hope he remembers it all his life. If he belonged to me I'd give him a good thrashing."

Stephen felt his mouth, his chin, his whole face jerking. He opened his mouth to take a breath, and tears and noise burst from him. "Stop that, fellow, stop that," said Uncle David, shaking him gently by the shoulders, but Stephen could not stop. He drew his breath again and it came back in a howl. Old Janet came to the door.

"Bring me some cold water," called Grandma. There was a flurry, a commotion, a breath of cool air from the hall, the door slammed, and Stephen heard his mother's voice. His howl died away, his breath sobbed and fluttered, he turned his dimmed eyes and saw her standing there. His heart turned over within him and he bleated like a lamb, "Maaaaama," running toward her. Uncle David stood back as Mama swooped in and fell on her knees beside Stephen. She gathered him to her and stood up with him in her arms.

"What are you doing to my baby?" she asked Uncle David in a thickened voice. "I should never have let him come here. I should have known better–"

"You always should know better," said Uncle David, "and you never do. And you never will. You haven't got it here," he told her, tapping his forehead.

"David," said Grandma, "that's your–"

"Yes, I know, she's my sister," said Uncle David. "I know it. But if she must run away and marry a–"

"Shut up," said Mama.

"And bring more like him into the world, let her keep them at home. I say let her keep–"

Mama set Stephen on the floor and, holding him by the hand, she said to Grandma all in a rush as if she were reading something, "Good-by, Mother. This is the last time, really the last. I can't bear it any longer. Say good-by to Stephen; you'll never see him again. You let this happen. It's your fault. You know David was a coward and a bully and a self-righteous little beast all his life and you never crossed him in anything. You let him bully me all my life and you let him slander my husband and call my baby a thief, and now this is the end. . . . He calls my baby a thief over a few horrible little balloons because he doesn't like my husband. . . ."

She was panting and staring about from one to the other. They were all standing. Now Grandma said, "Go home, daughter. Go away, David. I'm sick of your quarreling. I've never had a day's peace or comfort from either of you. I'm sick of you both. Now let me alone and stop this noise. Go away," said Grandma in a wavering voice. She took out her handkerchief and wiped first one eye and then the other and said, "All this hate, hate—what is it for? . . . So this is the way it turns out. Well, let me alone."

"You and your little advertising balloons," said Mama to Uncle David. "The big honest businessman advertises with balloons and if he loses one he'll be ruined. And your beastly little moral notions . . ."

Grandma went to the door to meet Old Janet, who handed her a glass of water. Grandma drank it all, standing there.

"Is your husband coming for you, or are you going home by yourself?" she asked Mama.

"I'm driving myself," said Mama in a far-away voice as if her mind had wandered. "You know he wouldn't set foot in this house."

"I should think not," said Uncle David.

"Come on, Stephen darling," said Mama. "It's far past his bedtime," she said, to no one in particular. "Imagine keeping a baby up to torture him about a few miserable little bits of colored rubber." She smiled at Uncle David with both rows of teeth as she passed him on the way to the door, keeping between him and Stephen. "Ah, where would we be without high moral standards," she said, and then to

Grandma, "Good night, Mother," in quite her usual voice. "I'll see you in a day or so."

"Yes, indeed," said Grandma cheerfully, coming out into the hall with Stephen and Mama. "Let me hear from you. Ring me up tomorrow. I hope you'll be feeling better."

"I feel very well now," said Mama brightly, laughing. She bent down and kissed Stephen. "Sleepy, darling? Papa's waiting to see you. Don't go to sleep until you've kissed your papa good night."

Stephen woke with a sharp jerk. He raised his head and put out his chin a little. "I don't want to go home," he said; "I want to go to school. I don't want to see Papa, I don't like him."

Mama laid her palm over his mouth softly. "Darling, don't."

Uncle David put his head out with a kind of snort. "There you are," he said. "There you've got a statement from headquarters."

Mama opened the door and ran, almost carrying Stephen. She ran across the sidewalk, jerking open the car door and dragging Stephen in after her. She spun the car around and dashed forward so sharply Stephen was almost flung out of the seat. He sat braced then with all his might, hands digging into the cushions. The car speeded up and the trees and houses whizzed by all flattened out. Stephen began suddenly to sing to himself, a quiet, inside song so Mama would not hear. He sang his new secret; it was a comfortable, sleepy song: "I hate Papa, I hate Mama, I hate Grandma, I hate Uncle David, I hate Old Janet, I hate Marjory, I hate Papa, I hate Mama . . ."

His head bobbed, leaned, came to rest on Mama's knee, eyes closed. Mama drew him closer and slowed down, driving with one hand.

A DAY'S WORK

A Day's Work

THE dull scrambling like a giant rat in the wall meant the dumb-waiter was on its way up, the janitress below hauling on the cable. Mrs. Halloran paused, thumped her iron on the board, and said, "There it is. Late. You could have put on your shoes and gone around the corner and brought the things an hour ago. I can't do everything."

Mr. Halloran pulled himself out of the chair, clutching the arms and heaving to his feet slowly, looking around as if he hoped to find crutches standing near. "Wearing out your socks, too," added Mrs. Halloran. "You ought either go barefoot outright or wear your shoes over your socks as God intended," she said. "Sock feet. What's the good of it, I'd like to know? Neither one thing nor the other."

She unrolled a salmon-colored chiffon nightgown with cream-colored lace and broad ribbons on it, gave it a light flirt in the air, and spread it on the board. "God's mercy, look at that indecent thing," she said. She thumped the iron again and pushed it back and forth over the rumpled cloth. "You might just set the things in the cupboard," she said, "and not leave them around on the floor. You might just."

Mr. Halloran took a sack of potatoes from the dumb-waiter

and started for the cupboard in the corner next the icebox. "You might as well take a load," said Mrs. Halloran. "There's no need on earth making a half-dozen trips back and forth. I'd think the poorest sort of man could well carry more than five pounds of potatoes at one time. But maybe not."

Her voice tapped on Mr. Halloran's ears like wood on wood. "Mind your business, will you?" he asked, not speaking to her directly. He carried on the argument with himself. "Oh, I couldn't do that, Mister Honey," he answered in a dull falsetto. "Don't ever ask me to think of such a thing, even. It wouldn't be right," he said, standing still with his knees bent, glaring bitterly over the potato sack at the scrawny strange woman he had never liked, that one standing there ironing clothes with a dirty look on her whole face like a suffering saint. "I may not be much good any more," he told her in his own voice, "but I still have got wits enough to take groceries off a dumb-waiter, mind you."

"That's a miracle," said Mrs. Halloran. "I'm thankful for that much."

"There's the telephone," said Mr. Halloran, sitting in the armchair again and taking his pipe out of his shirt pocket.

"I heard it as well," said Mrs. Halloran, sliding the iron up and down over the salmon-colored chiffon.

"It's for you, I've no further business in this world," said Mr. Halloran. His little greenish eyes glittered; he exposed his two sharp dogteeth in a grin.

"You could answer it. It could be the wrong number again or for somebody downstairs," said Mrs. Halloran, her flat voice going flatter, even.

"Let it go in any case," decided Mr. Halloran, "for my own part, that is." He struck a match on the arm of his chair, touched off his pipe, and drew in his first puff while the telephone went on with its nagging.

"It might be Maggie again," said Mrs. Halloran.

"Let her ring, then," said Mr. Halloran, settling back and crossing his legs.

"God help a man who won't answer the telephone when his own daughter calls up for a word," commented Mrs. Halloran to the ceiling. "And she in deep trouble, too, with her husband treating her like a dog about the money, and sitting out late nights in saloons with that crowd from the Little Tammany Association. He's getting into politics now with the McCorkery gang. No good will come of it, and I told her as much."

"She's no troubles at all, her man's a sharp fellow who will get ahead if she'll let him alone," said Mr. Halloran. "She's nothing to complain of, I could tell her. But what's a father?" Mr. Halloran cocked his head toward the window that opened on the brick-paved areaway and crowed like a rooster, "What's a father these days and who would heed his advice?"

"You needn't tell the neighbors, there's disgrace enough already," said Mrs. Halloran. She set the iron back on the gas ring and stepped out to the telephone on the first stair landing. Mr. Halloran leaned forward, his thin, red-haired hands hanging loosely between his knees, his warm pipe sending up its good decent smell right into his nose. The woman hated the pipe and the smell; she was a woman born to make any man miserable. Before the depression, while he still had a good job and prospects of a raise, before he went on relief, before she took in fancy washing and ironing, in the Good Days Before, God's pity, she didn't exactly keep her mouth shut, there wasn't a word known to man she couldn't find an answer for, but she knew which side her bread was buttered on, and put up with it. Now she was, you might say, buttering her own bread and she never forgot it for a minute. And it's her own fault we're not riding round today in a limousine with ash trays and a speaking tube and a cut-glass vase for flowers in it. It's what a man gets for marrying one of these holy women. Gerald McCorkery had told him as much, in the beginning.

"There's a girl will spend her time holding you down," Gerald had told him. "You're putting your head in a noose will strangle the life out of you. Heed the advice of one who wishes you well," said Gerald McCorkery. This was after he had barely set eyes on Lacey Mahaffy one Sunday morning in Coney Island. It was like McCorkery to see that in a flash, born judge of human nature that he was. He could look a man over, size him up, and there was an end to it.

And if the man didn't pass muster, McCorkery could ease him out in a way that man would never know how it happened. It was the secret of McCorkery's success in the world.

"This is Rosie, herself," said Gerald that Sunday in Coney Island. "Meet the future Mrs. Gerald J. McCorkery." Lacey Mahaffy's narrow face had gone sour as whey under her big straw hat. She barely nodded to Rosie, who gave Mr. Halloran a look that fairly undressed him right there. Mr. Halloran had thought, too, that McCorkery was picking a strange one; she was good-looking all right, but she had the smell of a regular little Fourteenth Street hustler if Halloran knew anything about women. "Come on," said McCorkery, his arm around Rosie's waist, "let's all go on the roller coaster." But Lacey would not. She said, "No, thank you. We didn't plan to stay, and we must go now." On the way home Mr. Halloran said, "Lacey, you judge too harshly. Maybe that's a nice girl at heart; hasn't had your opportunities." Lacey had turned upon him a face ugly as an angry cat's, and said, "She's a loose, low woman, and 'twas an insult to introduce her to me." It was a good while before the pretty fresh face that Mr. Halloran had fallen in love with returned to her.

Next day in Billy's Place, after three drinks each, McCorkery said, "Watch your step, Halloran; think of your future. There's a straight good girl I don't doubt, but she's no sort of mixer. A man getting into politics needs a wife who can meet all kinds. A man needs a woman knows how to loosen her corsets and sit easy."

Mrs. Halloran's voice was going on in the hall, a steady dry rattle like old newspapers blowing on a park bench. "I told you before it's no good coming to me with your troubles now. I warned you in time but you wouldn't listen. . . . I told you just how it would be, I tried my best. . . . No, you couldn't listen, you always knew better than your mother. . . . So now all you've got to do is stand by your married vows and make the best of it. . . . Now listen to me, if you want himself to do right you have to do right first. The woman has to do right first, and then if the man won't do right in turn it's no fault of hers. You do right whether he does wrong or no, just because he does wrong is no excuse for you."

"Ah, will you hear that?" Mr. Halloran asked the areaway in an awed voice. "There's a holy terror of a saint for you."

". . . the woman has to do right first, I'm telling you," said Mrs. Halloran into the telephone, "and then if he's a devil in spite of it, why she has to do right without any help from him." Her voice rose so the neighbors could get an earful if they wanted. "I know you from old, you're just like your father. You must be doing something wrong yourself or you wouldn't be in this fix. You're doing wrong this minute, calling over the telephone when you ought to be getting your work done. I've got an iron on, working over the dirty nightgowns of a kind of woman I wouldn't soil my foot on if I'd had a man to take care of me. So now you do up your housework and dress yourself and take a walk in the fresh air. . . ."

"A little fresh air never hurt anybody," commented Mr. Halloran loudly through the open window. "It's the gas gets a man down."

"Now listen to me, Maggie, that's not the way to talk over the public wires. Now you stop that crying and go and do your duty and don't be worrying me any more. And stop saying you're going to leave your husband, because where will you go, for one thing? Do you want to walk the streets or set up a laundry in your kitchen? You can't come back here, you'll stay with your husband where you belong. Don't be a fool, Maggie. You've got your living, and that's more than many a woman better than you has got. Yes, your father's all right. No, he's just sitting here, the same. God knows what's to become of us. But you know how he is, little he cares. . . . Now remember this, Maggie, if anything goes wrong with your married life it's your own fault and you needn't come here for sympathy. . . . I can't waste any more time on it. Good-by."

Mr. Halloran, his ears standing up for fear of missing a word, thought how Gerald J. McCorkery had gone straight on up the ladder with Rosie; and for every step the McCorkerys took upward, he, Michael Halloran, had taken a step downward with Lacey Mahaffy. They had started as greenhorns with the same chances at the same time and the same friends, but McCorkery had seized all his opportunities as they came, getting in steadily with the Big Shots in ward politics, one good thing leading to another. Rosie had known how to back him up and push him onward. The McCorkerys for years had invited him and Lacey to come over to the house and be sociable with the crowd, but Lacey would not.

"You can't run with that fast set and drink and stay out nights and hold your job," said Lacey, "and you should know better than to ask your wife to associate with that woman." Mr. Halloran had got into the habit of dropping around by himself, now and again, for McCorkery still liked him, was still willing to give him a foothold in the right places, still asked him for favors at election time. There was always a good lively crowd at the McCorkerys, wherever they were; for they moved ever so often to a better place, with more furniture. Rosie helped hand around the drinks, taking a few herself with a gay word for everybody. The player piano or the victrola would be going full blast, with everybody dancing, all looking like ready money and a bright future. He would get home late these evenings, back to the same little cold-water walk-up flat, because Lacey would not spend a dollar for show. It must all go into savings against old age, she said. He would be full of good food and drink, and find Lacey, in a bungalow apron, warming up the fried potatoes once more, cross and bitterly silent, hanging her head and frowning at the smell of liquor on his breath. "You might at least eat the potatoes when I've fried them and waited all this time," she would say. "Ah, eat them yourself, they're none of mine," he would snarl in his disappointment with her, and with the life she was leading him.

He had believed with all his heart for years that he would one day be manager of one of the G. and I. chain grocery stores he worked for, and when that hope gave out there was still his pension when they retired him. But two years before it was due they fired him, on account of the depression, they said. Overnight he was on the sidewalk, with no place to go with the news but home. "Jesus," said Mr. Halloran, still remembering that day after nearly seven years of idleness.

The depression hadn't touched McCorkery. He went on and on up the ladder, giving beefsteaks and beanfests and beer parties for the boys in Billy's Place, standing in with the right men and never missing a trick. At last the Gerald J. McCorkery Club chartered a whole boat for a big excursion up the river. It was a great day, with Lacey sitting at home sulking. After election Rosie had her picture in the papers, smiling at McCorkery; not fat exactly, just a fine figure of a woman with flowers pinned on her spotted fur coat, her teeth as good as ever. Oh, God, there was a girl for any man's money. Mr. Halloran saw out of his eye-corner the bony stooped back of Lacey Mahaffy, standing on one foot to rest the other like a tired old horse, leaning on her hands waiting for the iron to heat.

"That was Maggie, with her woes," she said.

"I hope you gave her some good advice," said Mr. Halloran. "I hope you told her to take up her hat and walk out on him."

Mrs. Halloran suspended the iron over a pair of pink satin panties. "I told her to do right and leave wrong-doing to the men," she said, in her voice like a phonograph record running down. "I told her to bear with the trouble God sends as her mother did before her."

Mr. Halloran gave a loud groan and knocked out his pipe on the chair arm. "You would ruin the world, woman, if you could, with your wicked soul, treating a new-married girl as if she had no home and no parents to come to. But she's no daughter of mine if she sits there peeling potatoes, letting a man run over her. No daughter of mine and I'll tell her so if she–"

"You know well she's your daughter, so hold your tongue," said Mrs. Halloran, "and if she heeded you she'd be walking the streets this minute. I brought her up an honest girl, and an honest woman she's going to be or I'll take her over my knee as I did when she was little. So there you are, Halloran."

Mr. Halloran leaned far back in his chair and felt along

the shelf above his head until his fingers touched a half-dollar he had noticed there. His hand closed over it, he got up instantly and looked about for his hat.

"Keep your daughter, Lacey Mahaffy," he said, "she's none of mine but the fruits of your long sinning with the Holy Ghost. And now I'm off for a little round and a couple of beers to keep my mind from dissolving entirely."

"You can't have that dollar you just now sneaked off the shelf," said Mrs. Halloran. "So you think I'm blind besides? Put it back where you found it. That's for our daily bread."

"I'm sick of bread daily," said Mr. Halloran, "I need beer. It was not a dollar, but a half-dollar as you know well."

"Whatever it was," said Mrs. Halloran, "it stands instead of a dollar to me. So just drop it."

"You've got tomorrow's potatoes sewed up in your pocket this minute, and God knows what sums in that black box wherever you hide it, besides the life savings," said Mr. Halloran. "I earned this half-dollar on relief, and it's going to be spent properly. And I'll not be back for supper, so you'll save on that, too. So long, Lacey Mahaffy, I'm off."

"If you never come back, it will be all the same," said Mrs. Halloran, not looking up.

"If I came back with a pocket full of money, you'd be glad to see me," said Mr. Halloran.

"It would want to be a great sum," said Mrs. Halloran.

Mr. Halloran shut the door behind him with a fine slam.

He strolled out into the clear fall weather, a late afternoon sun warming his neck and brightening the old red-brick, high-stooped houses of Perry Street. He would go after all these years to Billy's Place, he might find some luck there. He took his time, though, speaking to the neighbors as he went. "Good afternoon, Mr. Halloran." "Good afternoon to you, Missis Caffery." . . . "It's fine weather for the time of year, Mr. Gogarty." "It is indeed, Mr. Halloran." Mr. Halloran thrived on these civilities, he loved to flourish his hat and give a hearty good day like a man who has nothing on his mind. Ah, there was the young man from the G. and I. store around the corner. He knew what kind of job Mr. Halloran once held there. "Good day, Mr. Halloran." "Good day to you, Mr. McInerny, how's business holding up with you?" "Good for the times, Mr. Halloran, that's the best I can say." "Things are not getting any better, Mr. McInerny." "It's the truth we are all hanging on by the teeth now, Mr. Halloran."

Soothed by this acknowledgment of man's common misfortune Mr. Halloran greeted the young cop at the corner. The cop, with his quick eyesight, was snatching a read from a newspaper on the stand across the sidewalk. "How do you do, Young O'Fallon," asked Mr. Halloran, "is your business lively these days?"

"Quiet as the tomb itself on this block," said Young O'Fallon. "But that's a sad thing about Connolly, now." His eyes motioned toward the newspaper.

"Is he dead?" asked Mr. Halloran; "I haven't been out until now, I didn't see the papers."

"Ah, not yet," said Young O'Fallon, "but the G-men are after him, it looks they'll get him surely this time."

"Connolly in bad with the G-men? Holy Jesus," said Mr. Halloran, "who will they go after next? The meddlers."

"It's that numbers racket," said the cop. "What's the harm, I'd like to know? A man must get his money from somewhere when he's in politics. They oughta give him a chance."

"Connolly's a great fellow, God bless him, I hope he gives them the slip," said Mr. Halloran, "I hope he goes right through their hands like a greased pig."

"He's smart," said the cop. "That Connolly's a smooth one. He'll come out of it."

Ah, will he though? Mr. Halloran asked himself. Who is safe if Connolly goes under? Wait till I give Lacey Mahaffy the news about Connolly, I'll like seeing her face the first time in twenty years. Lacey kept saying, "A man is a downright fool must be a crook to get rich. Plenty of the best people get rich and do no harm by it. Look at the Connollys now, good practical Catholics with nine children and more to come if God sends them, and Mass every day, and they're rolling in wealth richer than your McCorkerys with all their wickedness." So there you are, Lacey Mahaffy, wrong again, and welcome to your pious Connollys. Still and all it was Connolly who had given Gerald McCorkery his start in the world; McCorkery had been publicity man and then campaign manager for Connolly, in the days when Connolly had Tammany in the palm of his hand and the sky was the limit. And McCorkery had begun at the beginning, God knows. He was running a little basement place first, rent almost nothing, where the boys of the Connolly Club and the Little Tammany Association, just the mere fringe of the district, you might say, could drop in for quiet evenings for a game and a drink along with the talk. Nothing low, nothing but what was customary, with the house taking a cut on the winnings and a fine profit on the liquor, and holding the crowd together. Many was the big plan hatched there came out well for everybody. For everybody but myself, and why was that? And when McCorkery says to me, "You can take over now and run the place for the McCorkery Club," ah, there was my chance and Lacey Mahaffy wouldn't hear of it, and with Maggie coming on just then it wouldn't do to excite her.

Mr. Halloran went on, following his feet that knew the way to Billy's Place, head down, not speaking to passersby any more, but talking it out with himself again, again. What a track to go over seeing clearly one by one the crossroads where he might have taken a different turn that would have changed all his fortunes; but no, he had gone the other way and now it was too late. She wouldn't say a thing but "It's not right and you know it, Halloran," so what could a man do in all? Ah, you could have gone on with your rightful affairs like any other man, Halloran, it's not the woman's place to decide such things; she'd have come round once she saw the money, or a good whack on the backsides would have put her in her place. Never had mortal woman needed a good walloping worse than Lacey Mahaffy, but he could never find it in his heart to give it to her for her own good. That was just another of your many mistakes, Halloran. But there was always the life-long job with the G. and I. and peace in the house more or less. Many a man envied me in those days I remember, and I was resting easy on the savings and knowing with that and the pension I could finish out my life with some little business of my own. "What came of that?" Mr. Halloran inquired in a low voice, looking around him. Nobody answered. You know well what came of it, Halloran. You were fired out like a delivery boy, two years before your time was out. Why did you sit there watching the trick being played on others before you, knowing well it could happen to you and never quite believing what you saw with your own eyes? G. and I. gave me my start, when I was green in this country, and they were my own kind or I thought so. Well, it's done now. Yes, it's done now, but there was all the years you could have cashed in on the numbers game with the best of them, helping collect the protection money and taking your cut. You could have had a fortune by now in Lacey's name, safe in the bank. It was good quiet profit and none the wiser. But they're wiser now, Halloran, don't forget; still it's a lump of grief and disappointment to swallow all the same. The game's up with Connolly, maybe; Lacey Mahaffy had said, "Numbers is just another way of stealing from the poor, and you weren't born to be a thief like that McCorkery." Ah, God, no, Halloran, you were born to rot on relief and maybe that's honest enough for her. That Lacey— A fortune in her name would have been no good to me whatever. She's got all the savings tied up, such as they are, she'll pinch and she'll starve, she'll wash dirty clothes first, she won't give up a penny to live on. She has stood in my way, McCorkery, like a skeleton rattling its bones, and you were right about her, she has been my ruin. "Ah, it's not too late yet, Halloran," said McCorkery, appearing plain as day inside Mr. Halloran's head with the same old face and way with him. "Never say die, Halloran. Elections are coming on again, it's a busy time for all, there's work to be done and you're the very man I'm looking for. Why didn't you come to me sooner, you know I never forget an old friend. You don't deserve your ill fortune, Halloran," McCorkery told him; "I said so to others and I say it now to your face, never did man deserve more of the world than you, Halloran, but the truth is, there's not always enough good luck to go round; but it's your turn now, and I've got a job for you up to your abilities at last. For a man like you, there's nothing to it at all, you can toss it off with one hand tied, Halloran, and good money in it. Organization work, just among your own neighbors, where you're known and respected for a man of your word and an old friend of Gerald McCorkery. Now look, Halloran," said Gerald McCorkery, tipping him the wink, "do I need to say more? It's voters in large numbers we're after, Halloran, and you're to bring them in, alive or dead. Keep your eye on the situation at all times and get in touch with me when necessary. And name your figure in the way of money. And come up to the house sometimes, Halloran, why don't you? Rosie has asked me a hundred times, 'Whatever went with Halloran, the life of the party?' That's the way you stand with Rosie, Halloran. We're in a two-story flat now with green velvet curtains and carpets you can sink to your shoetops in, and there's no reason at all why you shouldn't have the same kind of place if you want it. With your gifts, you were never meant to be a poor man."

Ah, but Lacey Mahaffy wouldn't have it, maybe. "Then get yourself another sort of woman, Halloran, you're a good man still, find yourself a woman like Rosie to snuggle down with at night." Yes, but McCorkery, you forget that Lacey Mahaffy had legs and hair and eyes and a complexion fit for a chorus girl. But would she do anything with them? Never. Would you believe there was a woman wouldn't take off all her clothes at once even to bathe herself? What a hateful thing she was with her evil mind thinking everything was a sin, and never giving a man a chance to show himself a man in any way. But she's faded away now, her mean soul shows out all over her, she's ugly as sin itself now, McCorkery. "It's what I told you would happen," said McCorkery, "but now with the job and the money you can go your ways and let Lacey Mahaffy go hers." I'll do it, McCorkery. "And forget about Connolly. Just remember I'm my own man and always was. Connolly's finished, but I'm not. Stronger than ever, Halloran, with Connolly out of the way. I saw this coming long ever ago, Halloran, I got clear of it. They don't catch McCorkery with his pants down, Halloran. And I almost forgot . . . Here's something for the running expenses to start. Take this for the present, and there's more to come. . . ."

Mr. Halloran stopped short, a familiar smell floated under his nose: the warm beer-and-beefsteak smell of Billy's Place, sawdust and onions, like any other bar maybe, but with something of its own besides. The talk within him stopped also as if a hand had been laid on his mind. He drew his fist out of his pocket almost expecting to find green money in it. The half dollar was in his palm. "I'll stay while it lasts and hope McCorkery will come in."

The moment he stepped inside his eye lighted on McCorkery standing at the bar pouring his own drink from the bottle before him. Billy was mopping the bar before him idly, and his eye, swimming toward Halloran, looked like an oyster in its own juice. McCorkery saw him too. "Well, blow me down, " he said, in a voice that had almost lost its old County Mayo ring, "if it ain't my old sidekick from the G. and I. Step right up, Halloran," he said, his poker-face as good as ever, no man ever saw Gerald McCorkery surprised at anything. "Step up and name your choice."

Mr. Halloran glowed suddenly with the warmth around the heart he always had at the sight of McCorkery, he couldn't put a name on it, but there was something about the man. Ah, it was Gerald all right, the same, who never forgot a friend and never seemed to care whether a man was rich or poor, with his face of granite and his eyes like blue agates in his head, a rock of a man surely. There he was, saying "Step right up," as if they had parted only yesterday; portly and solid in his expensive-looking clothes, as always; his hat a darker gray than his suit, with a devil-may-care roll to the brim, but nothing sporting, mind you. All first-rate, well made, and the right thing for him, more power to him. Mr. Halloran said, "Ah, McCorkery, you're the one man on this round earth I hoped to see today, but I says to myself, maybe he doesn't come round to Billy's Place so much nowadays."

"And why not?" asked McCorkery, "I've been coming around to Billy's Place for twenty-five years now, it's still headquarters for the old guard of the McCorkery Club, Halloran." He took in Mr. Halloran from head to foot in a flash of a glance and turned toward the bottle.

"I was going to have a beer," said Mr. Halloran, "but the smell of that whiskey changes my mind for me." McCorkery poured a second glass, they lifted the drinks with an identical crook of the elbow, a flick of the wrist at each other.

"Here's to crime," said McCorkery, and "Here's looking at you," said Mr. Halloran, merrily. Ah, to hell with it, he was back where he belonged, in good company. He put his foot on the rail and snapped down his whiskey, and no sooner was his glass on the bar than McCorkery was filling it again. "Just time for a few quick ones," he said, "before the boys get here." Mr. Halloran downed that one, too, before he noticed that McCorkery hadn't filled his own glass. "I'm ahead of you," said McCorkery, "I'll skip this one."

There was a short pause, a silence fell around them that seemed to ooze like a fog from somewhere deep in McCorkery, it was suddenly as if he had not really been there at all, or hadn't uttered a word. Then he said outright: "Well, Halloran, let's have it. What's on your mind?" And he poured two more drinks. That was McCorkery all over, reading your thoughts and coming straight to the point.

Mr. Halloran closed his hand round his glass and peered into the little pool of whiskey. "Maybe we could sit down," he said, feeling weak-kneed all at once. McCorkery took the bottle and moved over to the nearest table. He sat facing the door, his look straying there now and then, but he had a set, listening face as if he was ready to hear anything.

"You know what I've had at home all these years," began Mr. Halloran, solemnly, and paused.

"Oh, God, yes," said McCorkery with simple good-fellowship. "How is herself these days?"

"Worse than ever," said Mr. Halloran, "but that's not it."

"What is it, then, Halloran?" asked McCorkery, pouring drinks. "You know well you can speak out your mind to me. Is it a loan?"

"No," said Mr. Halloran. "It's a job."

"Now that's a different matter," said McCorkery. "What kind of a job?"

Mr. Halloran, his head sunk between his shoulders, saw McCorkery wave a hand and nod at half a dozen men who came in and ranged themselves along the bar. "Some of the boys," said McCorkery. "Go on." His face was tougher, and quieter, as if the drink gave him a firm hold on himself. Mr. Halloran said what he had planned to say, had said already on the way down, and it still sounded reasonable and right to him. McCorkery waited until he had finished, and got up, putting a hand on Mr. Halloran's shoulder. "Stay where you are, and help yourself," he said, giving the bottle a little push, "and anything else you want, Halloran, order it on me. I'll be back in a few minutes, and you know I'll help you out if I can."

Halloran understood everything but it was through a soft warm fog, and he hardly noticed when McCorkery passed him again with the men, all in that creepy quiet way like footpads on a dark street. They went into the back room, the door opened on a bright light and closed again, and Mr. Halloran reached for the bottle to help himself wait until McCorkery should come again bringing the good word. He felt comfortable and easy as if he hadn't a bone or muscle in him, but his elbow slipped off the table once or twice and he upset his drink on his sleeve. Ah, McCorkery, is it the whole family you're taking on with the jobs? For my Maggie's husband is in now with the Little Tammany Association. "There's a bright lad will go far and I've got my eye on him, Halloran," said the friendly voice of McCorkery in his mind, and the brown face, softer than he remembered it, came up clearly behind his closed eyes.

"Ah, well, it's like myself beginning all over again in him," said Mr. Halloran, aloud, "besides my own job that I might have had all this time if I'd just come to see you sooner."

"True for you," said McCorkery in a merry County Mayo voice, inside Mr. Halloran's head, "and now let's drink to the gay future for old times' sake and be damned to Lacey Mahaffy." Mr. Halloran reached for the bottle but it skipped sideways, rolled out of reach like a creature, and exploded at his feet. When he stood up the chair fell backward from under him. He leaned on the table and it folded up under his hands like cardboard.

"Wait now, take it easy," said McCorkery, and there he

was, real enough, holding Mr. Halloran braced on the one side, motioning with his hand to the boys in the back room, who came out quietly and took hold of Mr. Halloran, some of them, on the other side. Their faces were all Irish, but not an Irishman Mr. Halloran knew in the lot, and he did not like any face he saw. "Let me be," he said with dignity, "I came here to see Gerald J. McCorkery, a friend of mine from old times, and let not a thug among you lay a finger upon me."

"Come on, Big Shot," said one of the younger men, in a voice like a file grating, "come on now, it's time to go."

"That's a fine low lot you've picked to run with, McCorkery," said Mr. Halloran, bracing his heels against the slow weight they put upon him toward the door, "I wouldn't trust one of them far as I could throw him by the tail."

"All right, all right, Halloran," said McCorkery. "Come on with me. Lay off him, Finnegan." He was leaning over Mr. Halloran and pressing something into his right hand. It was money, a neat little roll of it, good smooth thick money, no other feel like it in the world, you couldn't mistake it. Ah, he'd have an argument to show Lacey Mahaffy would knock her off her feet. Honest money with a job to back it up. "You'll stand by your given word, McCorkery, as ever?" he asked, peering into the rock-colored face above him, his feet weaving a dance under him, his heart ready to break with gratitude.

"Ah, sure, sure," said McCorkery in a loud hearty voice with a kind of curse in it. "Crisakes, get on with him, do." Mr. Halloran found himself eased into a taxicab at the curb, with McCorkery speaking to the driver and giving him money. "So long, Big Shot," said one of the thug faces, and the taxicab door thumped to. Mr. Halloran bobbed about on the seat for a while, trying to think. He leaned forward and spoke to the driver. "Take me to my friend Gerald J. McCorkery's house," he said, "I've got important business. Don't pay any attention to what he said. Take me to his house."

"Yeah?" said the driver, without turning his head. "Well, here's where you get out, see? Right here." He reached back and opened the door. And sure enough, Mr. Halloran was standing on the sidewalk in front of the flat in Perry Street, alone except for the rows of garbage cans, the taxicab hooting its way around the corner, and a cop coming toward him, plainly to be seen under the street light.

"You should cast your vote for McCorkery, the poor man's friend," Mr. Halloran told the cop, "McCorkery's the man who will get us all off the spot. Stands by his old friends like a maniac. Got a wife named Rosie. Vote for McCorkery," said Mr. Halloran, working hard at his job, "and you'll be Chief of the Force when Halloran says the word."

"To hell with McCorkery, that stooge," said the cop, his mouth square and sour with the things he said and the things he saw and did every night on that beat. "There you are drunk again, Halloran, shame to you, with Lacey Mahaffy working her heart out over the washboard to buy your beer."

"It wasn't beer and she didn't buy it, mind you," said Mr. Halloran, "and what do you know about Lacey Mahaffy?"

"I knew her from old when I used to run errands for St. Veronica's Altar Society," said the cop, "and she was a great one, even then. Nothing good enough."

"It's the same today," said Mr. Halloran, almost sober for a moment.

"Well, go on up now and stay up till you're fit to be seen," said the cop, censoriously.

"You're Johnny Maginnis," said Mr. Halloran, "I know you well."

"You should know me by now," said the cop.

Mr. Halloran worked his way upstairs partly on his hands and knees, but once at his own door he stood up, gave a great blow on the panel with his fist, turned the knob and surged in like a wave after the door itself, holding out the money toward Mrs. Halloran, who had finished ironing and was at her mending.

She got up very slowly, her bony hand over her mouth, her eyes starting out at what she saw. "Ah, did you steal it?" she asked. "Did you kill somebody for that?" the words grated up from her throat in a dark whisper. Mr. Halloran glared back at her in fear.

"Suffering Saints, Lacey Mahaffy," he shouted until the whole houseful could hear him, "haven't ye any mind at all that you can't see your husband has had a turn of fortune and a job and times are changed from tonight? Stealing, is it? That's for your great friends the Connollys with their religion. Connolly steals, but Halloran is an honest man with a job in the McCorkery Club, and money in pocket."

"McCorkery, is it?" said Mrs. Halloran, loudly too. "Ah, so there's the whole family, young and old, wicked and innocent, taking their bread from McCorkery, at last. Well, it's no bread of mine, I'll earn my own as I have, you can keep your dirty money to yourself, Halloran, mind you I mean it."

"Great God, woman," moaned Mr. Halloran, and he tottered from the door to the table, to the ironing board, and stood there, ready to weep with rage, "haven't you a soul even that you won't come along with your husband when he's riding to riches and glory on the Tiger's back itself, with everything for the taking and no questions asked?"

"Yes, I have a soul," cried Mrs. Halloran, clenching her fists, her hair flying. "Surely I have a soul and I'll save it yet in spite of you. . . ."

She was standing there before him in a kind of faded gingham winding sheet, with her dead hands upraised, her dead eyes blind but fixed upon him, her voice coming up hollow from the deep tomb, her throat thick with grave damp. The ghost of Lacey Mahaffy was threatening him, it came nearer, growing taller as it came, the face changing to a demon's face with a fixed glassy grin. "It's all that drink on an empty stomach," said the ghost, in a hoarse growl. Mr. Halloran fetched a yell of horror right out of his very boots, and seized the flatiron from the board. "Ah, God damn you, Lacey Mahaffy, you devil, keep away, keep away," he howled, but she advanced on air, grinning and growling. He raised the flatiron and hurled it without aiming, and the specter, whoever it was, whatever it was, sank and was gone. He did not look, but broke out of the room and was back on the sidewalk before he knew he had meant to go there. Maginnis came up at once. "Hey there now, Halloran," he said, "I mean business this time. You get back upstairs or I'll run you in. Come along now, I'll help you get there this time, and that's the last of it. On relief the way you are, and drinking your head off."

Mr. Halloran suddenly felt calm, collected; he would take Maginnis up and show him just what had happened. "I'm not on relief any more, and if you want any trouble, just call on my friend, McCorkery. He'll tell you who I am."

"McCorkery can't tell me anything about you I don't know already," said Maginnis. "Stand up there now." For Halloran wanted to go up again on his hands and knees.

"Let a man be," said Mr. Halloran, trying to sit on the cop's feet. "I killed Lacey Mahaffy at last, you'll be pleased to hear," he said, looking up into the cop's face. "It was high time and past. But I did not steal the money."

"Well, ain't that just too bad," said the cop, hauling him up under the arms. "Chees, why'n't you make a good job while you had the chance? Stand up now. Ah, hell with it, stand up or I'll sock you one."

Mr. Halloran said, "Well, you don't believe it so wait and see."

At that moment they both glanced upward and saw Mrs. Halloran coming downstairs. She was holding to the rail, and even in the speckled hall-light they could see a great lumpy clout of flesh standing out on her forehead, all colors. She stopped, and seemed not at all surprised.

"So there you are, Officer Maginnis," she said. "Bring him up."

"That's a fine welt you've got over your eye this time, Mrs. Halloran," commented Officer Maginnis, politely.

"I fell and hit my head on the ironing board," said Mrs. Halloran. "It comes of overwork and worry, day and night. A dead faint, Officer Maginnis. Watch your big feet there, you thriving, natural fool," she added to Mr. Halloran. "He's got a job now, you mightn't believe it, Officer Maginnis, but it's true. Bring him on up, and thank you."

She went ahead of them, opened the door, and led the way to the bedroom through the kitchen, turned back the covers, and Officer Maginnis dumped Mr. Halloran among the quilts and pillows. Mr. Halloran rolled over with a deep groan and shut his eyes.

"Many thanks to you, Officer Maginnis," said Mrs. Halloran.

"Don't mention it, Mrs. Halloran," said Officer Maginnis.

When the door was shut and locked, Mrs. Halloran went and dipped a large bath towel under the kitchen tap. She wrung it out and tied several good hard knots in one end and tried it out with a whack on the edge of the table. She walked in and stood over the bed and brought the knotted towel down in Mr. Halloran's face with all her might. He stirred and muttered, ill at ease. "That's for the flatiron, Halloran," she told him, in a cautious voice as if she were talking to herself, and whack, down came the towel again. "That's for the half-dollar," she said, and whack, "that's for your drunkenness—" Her arm swung around regularly, ending with a heavy thud on the face that was beginning to squirm, gasp, lift itself from the pillow and fall back again, in a puzzled kind of torment. "For your sock feet," Mrs. Halloran told him, whack, "and your laziness, and this is for missing Mass and"—here she swung half a dozen times—"that is for your daughter and your part in her. . . ."

She stood back breathless, the lump on her forehead burning in its furious colors. When Mr. Halloran attempted to rise, shielding his head with his arms, she gave him a push and he fell back again. "Stay there and don't give me a word," said Mrs. Halloran. He pulled the pillow over his face and subsided again, this time for good.

Mrs. Halloran moved about very deliberately. She tied the wet towel around her head, the knotted end hanging over her shoulder. Her hand ran into her apron pocket and came out again with the money. There was a five-dollar bill with three one-dollar bills rolled in it, and the half-dollar she had thought spent long since. "A poor start, but something," she said, and opened the cupboard door with a long key. Reaching in, she pulled a loosely fitted board out of the wall, and removed a black-painted metal box. She unlocked this, took out one five-cent piece from a welter of notes and coins. She then placed the new money in the box, locked it, put it away, replaced the board, shut the cupboard door and locked that. She went out to the telephone, dropped the nickel in the slot, asked for a number, and waited.

"Is that you, Maggie? Well, are things any better with you now? I'm glad to hear it. It's late to be calling, but there's news about your father. No, no, nothing of that kind, he's got a job. I said a *job*. Yes, at last, after all my urging him onward. . . . I've got him bedded down to sleep it off so he'll be ready for work tomorrow. . . . Yes, it's political work, toward the election time, with Gerald McCorkery. But that's no harm, getting votes and all, he'll be in the open air and it doesn't mean I'll have to associate with low people, now or ever. It's clean enough work, with good pay; if it's not just what I prayed for, still it beats nothing, Maggie. After all my trying . . . it's like a miracle. You see what can be done with patience and doing your duty, Maggie. Now mind you do as well by your own husband."

THE LEANING TOWER

The Leaning Tower

EARLY one morning on his sixth day in Berlin, on the twenty-seventh of December, 1931, Charles Upton left his dull little hotel in Hedemanstrasse and escaped to the café across the street. The air of the hotel was mysteriously oppressive to him; a yellow-faced woman and an ill-tempered looking fat man were the proprietors, and they seemed to be in perpetual conspiracy of some sort before open linen closets, in a corner of the dining room, along the halls, or over the account books behind a varnished desk in the lobby. His room was dark, airless, cold, and once when he had supper there, small white worms had come squirming out of the liver sausage on his plate. It was too expensive for him, besides, and he had decided to change. The café was dull, too, but with a look of thrifty cheerfulness, and Charles had pleasant associations with it. He had spent his first Christmas Eve in Europe there, among a small company of amiable noisy people who all seemed, by their conversation, to work in the same factory. No one but the old waiter had spoken to him, but the others talked heartily among themselves in what Charles recognized already as the Berlin accent, blunt, full of a wooden kind of clucking and quacking and explosive hissing.

During his voyage on a German boat, the German passengers had taken occasion to praise each his own province in the matter of speech, but not one of them said a good word for Berlin in the matter, not even the Berliners themselves. Charles, who had learned his German partly from textbooks, partly from phonograph records, a little from listening to the Germans in his native town, heard with pleasure the tough speech, drank his beer slowly, the good dark beer that already had spoiled his taste for any other, and rather determinedly began to persuade himself that he had not made a mistake. Yes, Germany was the right place for him, Berlin was the city, Kuno had been right and would be glad if he could know his friend was here at last.

He had thought, fitfully, of Kuno all that Christmas Eve, instead of his parents, who wrote long letters timed to reach him at the holiday saying how gloomy they would be without him. He had sent them a cable and had meant to think of them constantly, but he had not. Again, sitting in the café in the morning, with a map of the city and a pamphlet for tourists containing a list of pensions with prices, he found himself remembering Kuno in rather sudden, unexpected pictures, even seeing himself as he was then, and these flashes of memory came against still other flashes, and back somewhere in the dark of his mind was the whole story, whatever it was. He and Kuno did not remember when they had not known each other. Their first recollection was of standing next each other in a row of children like themselves, singing, or some such nonsense—it must have been kindergarten. They had lived and had gone to school together in an old small city in Texas settled early by the Spaniards. Mexicans, Spaniards, Germans, and Americans mostly from Kentucky had mingled there more or less comfortably for several generations, and though they were all equally citizens, the Spaniards, who were mainly rich and showy, went back to visit Spain from time to time. The Germans went back to Germany and the Mexicans, who lived mostly by themselves in the old quarter, went back to Mexico when they could afford it. Only the Kentuckians stayed where they were, rarely did any of them even go back to Kentucky, and though Charles heard them talk about the place often and lovingly, it seemed farther away and less desirable than Germany, because Kuno went there with his parents.

Though Kuno's mother was said to be a Baroness in Germany, in Texas she was the wife of a prosperous merchant, a furniture dealer. The Kentuckians, who were gradually starving on the land, thought the land the only honorable means to a living, unless one entered a profession; and Charles, whose family made their living, such as it was, from a blackland farm, wondered at the pride with which Kuno would lead him past his father's shop windows to show him the latest display of fashionable, highly polished and stuffed furniture. Looking through the broad clear window into the depths of the shop, Mr. Hillentafel, Kuno's father, could be seen dimly, pencil behind his ear, in his black alpaca coat, his head inclined attentively before a customer. Charles, used to seeing his father on horseback, or standing about the barns with the Negroes, looking at the animals, or walking the fields in his big boots, or riding on the cast iron seat of a plow or harrow, felt he would have been ashamed to see his father in a store, following someone about trying to sell him something. The only time he had ever felt like fighting with Kuno was after Kuno had returned from the second visit to Germany, when they were both about eight years old. Kuno one day spoke contemptuously of farmers, calling them a name in German which Charles did not understand. "They're as good as storekeepers," Charles said in a fury. "Your papa's just a storekeeper." Kuno had shouted back, "My mother is a Baroness, and we were all born in Germany, so we would be Germans. In Germany only low-down people work on farms."

"Well, if you are German, why don't you go and live there?" Charles had shouted back, and Kuno had said very proudly, "There is a big war there, and they wanted to keep my mama and my papa and all of us there, but we had to come back." Kuno then began to explain in a mystified way how they almost hadn't got back; they had almost got locked up in a prison somewhere, but some big important people came and got them out, and in the exciting but confused tale which followed, Charles forgot his quarrel with Kuno. "It was because my mother is a Baroness," Kuno said. "That is why we got away."

But after the war, Mr. Hillentafel took his family back to Germany for a few months every two years, and Kuno's postcards, with their foreign stamps, coming from far-off places like Bremen and Wiesbaden and Mannheim and Heidelberg and Berlin, had brought the great world across the sea, the blue silent deep world of Europe, straight to Charles' door. When he returned, Kuno always had new, odd but serious-looking clothes. He brought fascinating mechanical toys; and later, neckties of strange rich material, coats with stitched pockets, and blunt-toed thick shoes of light brown leather, all made by hand, he said. Kuno would say in the little accent he always brought back and which took several weeks to wear off, "No, but if you don't go to Berlin, you miss everything. We waste time always in those horrid little places, Mannheim and so on, we have to visit with our dull relatives, of course, they are stuck to the necks there, but in Berlin . . ." and he would talk for hours about Berlin until Charles in his imagination saw it as a great shimmering city of castles towering in misty light. How had he got such an image? Kuno had said only, "The streets are polished like a table top and they are as wide as—" he would measure with his eye the street they were walking in, a very narrow crooked dirty little street in an old colonial Spanish city—

"oh, five times as wide as this. And the buildings–" he would glance up, disgust in his face for the flat roofs lowering over them–"they are all of stone and marble and are carved, carved all over, with pillars and statues everywhere and staircases wider than a house, winding . . ."

"My father says," Charles said once, trying to keep abreast of all this knowledge of grandeur, "in Mexico the horses have silver bridles."

"I don't believe it," said Kuno, "and if they do, it's nonsense. Who would be so silly as to bridle a horse with silver? But in Berlin, there are marble houses carved all over with roses, loops of roses . . ."

"That sounds silly too," said Charles, but feebly, because it did not sound silly at all, any more than did the silver bridles on the horses of Mexico. Those things were what he would like, what he most longed to see, and he said, easily, "I'll go there too, some day."

Kuno played the violin, and went twice a week to a stern old German teacher who cracked him over the head with a bow when he made mistakes; and his parents forced him to practice three hours every day. Charles wanted to paint and draw, but his parents thought he wasted time at it when he could have been doing something useful, like studying, so he merely scratched around with charcoal on odd sheets of paper, or dabbled for hours in some retired spot with brushes that shed hairs in his poorly equipped paint boxes. On the fourth or fifth voyage to Germany, when Kuno was about fifteen, he died there and was buried in Wiesbaden. His parents, bringing back, beside the elder brother and sister, a new baby, the second within Charles' memory, were very silent on the subject. They were all fair, tall, lightboned, rather lifeless people, and Charles, who had no friendship with any of them but Kuno, hardly saw them or thought of them any more.

Charles, sitting in the café, trying to put his mind on the necessity for beginning a search for a cheaper room, thought, If it hadn't been for Kuno I should never have come here. I would have gone to Paris, or to Madrid. Maybe I should have gone to Mexico. That's a good place for painters. . . . This is not right. There is something wrong with the shapes, or the light, or something. . . .

His father had been to Mexico when he was young and had told Charles long stories, but Charles had never listened to him as he had to Kuno. So here he was, trying to be a painter, even believing by now that he was really going to be a good one, and he had come, as he believed, on a reasoned decision strictly his own. In his new, vague, almost shapeless misgivings, his half-acknowledged disappointment in the place —what was it?—he began to understand that he had come to Berlin because Kuno had made it seem the one desirable place to be. He hardly ever thought of Kuno any more, or had not for a long time, except simply as dead, though that went on being hard to believe; still it was just those colored postcards of Kuno's and those stories, and the way Kuno had felt then, and had made him feel, that had brought him here. Soberly facing facts, he decided that wasn't enough reason, not half enough. But still he decided also to stay, if he possibly could.

It would be four days until New Year's, and Charles began to think seriously about money. The next boat would bring him a check from his father, who had decided, in a kind of mixed despair and pride in his son's talent, to help him. Charles, keeping accounts in a book, had resolved it should all be repaid. The editor of a small art magazine was publishing a series of his drawings, and was going to pay for them. If these failed, he saw clearly that even beer for his New Year's celebration would be out of the question. Still, at one time or another, the sooner the better, there would be a boat coming from America, and it would bring him money, not much, but enough to keep him going. Meantime, he thought of his expensive camera, which a Kentucky aunt had given him, and decided instantly to pawn it. He also had his grandfather's big gold watch. Why, he was rich. This settled, the question went out of his mind, except for a faint uneasiness as to where his money had gone. In the days before Christmas he had dropped, rather carelessly, without counting, small change into the hats and outspread handkerchiefs of the men along the streets, who were making the most of their holiday licenses to beg. Some of them begged in orderly groups, singing carols familiar to him from the days when his parents took him to the German Singing Society at home: "Heilige Nacht," "O Tannenbaum," Martin Luther's "Cradle Song," in the familiar singing society voices, even, full, melodious. They had stood there with their ragged shoes sunk in the slushy snow, starving and blue-nosed, singing in their mourning voices, accepting coins with grave nods, keeping their eyes fixed on each other as they beat time softly with their hands.

Others stood alone, and these the most miserable, each man isolated in his incurable misfortune. Those blinded or otherwise mutilated in the war wore a certain band on their sleeves to prove that they had more than any others earned the right to beg, and merited special charity. Charles, with his almost empty pockets, nothing in them except the future, which he felt he owned, saw a tall young man so emaciated his teeth stood out in ridges under the mottled tight skin of his cheeks, standing at the curb with a placard around his neck which read: "I will take any work you can offer." Almost furtively, Charles slipped a mark into the limp hollowed palm, then stepped into the doorway near by, and sheltered by fir trees piled before a shop, their sweet odor in his nostrils, with cold fingers he sketched hastily the stiff figure in its abject garments, surmounted by that skull of famine.

He walked on thinking it would be a relief when the

necessity for appearing to celebrate something was over, remembering with the present smell of freshly cut fir the smell of apples along the curbs of New York streets, while he was roaming about the picture galleries waiting for his boat. Men stood shivering by the fruit, or patrolled the sidewalks, saying, "Brother, can you spare a dime?" The saying had become famous, a catchword, at once. Then almost overnight the whole thing had become simply a picturesque aspect of the times, a piece of local color, a current fad. Even if the plight of the men was real, it was not going to last; the breadlines were only temporary, the newspapers insisted, and gave strange wonderful far-fetched reasons for the situation, as if it had been a phenomenon of nature, like an earthquake, or a cloudburst.

Here, Charles could see, the misery was acknowledged as real and the sufferers seemed to know they had no reason for hope. There was none of the raffish manner of the apple-sellers, but just complete hopelessness and utter endurance. . . . Yet back of them the windows along Kurfürstendamm and Unter den Linden were filled with fine wools and furs and overcoats and great shining motor cars. Charles, walking and gazing, compared them with the New York windows back of the apple sellers and the beggars. They were by no means so fine, but where were the buyers? In New York the buyers streamed gaily in and out of shops, dropping dimes into extended hands. Here, a few dully dressed persons stood and stared, but when he glanced in, the shops were almost empty. The streets were full of young people, lean and tough, boys and girls alike dressed in leather jackets or a kind of uniform blue ski suit, who whizzed about the streets on bicycles without a glance at the windows. Charles saw them carrying skis on their shoulders, shouting and laughing in groups, getting away to the mountains over the weekend. He watched them enviously; maybe if he stayed on long enough he would know some of them, he would be riding a bicycle and going away for the skiing, too. It seemed unlikely, though.

He would wander on, and the thicker the crowd in which he found himself, the more alien he felt himself to be. He had watched a group of middle-aged men and women who were gathered in silence before two adjoining windows, gazing silently at displays of toy pigs and sugar pigs. These persons were all strangely of a kind, and strangely the most prevalent type. The streets were full of them—enormous waddling women with short legs and ill-humored faces, and round-headed men with great rolls of fat across the backs of their necks, who seemed to support their swollen bellies with an effort that drew their shoulders forward. Nearly all of them were leading their slender, overbred, short-legged dogs in pairs on fancy leashes. The dogs wore their winter clothes: wool sweaters, fur ruffs, and fleece-lined rubber boots. The creatures whined and complained and shivered, and their owners lifted them up tenderly to show them the pigs.

In one window there were sausages, hams, bacon, small pink chops; all pig, real pig, fresh, smoked, salted, baked, roasted, pickled, spiced, and jellied. In the other were dainty artificial pigs, almond paste pigs, pink sugar chops, chocolate sausages, tiny hams and bacons of melting cream streaked and colored to the very life. Among the tinsel and lace paper, at the back were still other kinds of pigs: plush pigs, black velvet pigs, spotted cotton pigs, metal and wooden mechanical pigs, all with frolicsome curled tails and appealing infant faces.

With their nervous dogs wailing in their arms, the people, shameless mounds of fat, stood in a trance of pig worship, gazing with eyes damp with admiration and appetite. They resembled the most unkind caricatures of themselves, but they were the very kind of people that Holbein and Dürer and Urs Graf had drawn, too: not vaguely, but positively like, their late-medieval faces full of hallucinated malice and a kind of sluggish but intense cruelty that worked its way up from their depths slowly through the layers of helpless gluttonous fat.

The thin snow continued to fall and whiten rounded shoulders and lumpy hat brims. Charles, feeling the flakes inside his collar, had walked on with intention to get away from the spectacle which struck him as revolting. He had walked on into Friedrichstrasse, where, in the early evening, the thin streetwalkers came out and moved rather swiftly in the middle of the pavement, and though they all appeared to be going somewhere, they never left each one her own certain fixed station. They seemed quite unapproachable to Charles in their black lace skirts and high gilded heels, their feathered hats and grease paint. On his first evening in Berlin a young unsmiling one had spoken to him, inviting him without enthusiasm to come with her. He had stammered a phrase which he hoped meant, "I haven't time now," fearing that she would insist. She had given him a serious, appraising glance, saw, to his shame, that the market was no good, and had turned away with an indifferent, "Well, good evening." At home, his adventures had all been with girls he knew, and the element of chance had always been present. Any given occasion might go off very well, and it might not; he felt he had learned a lot from what he described to himself as the block and tackle, balance and check, trial and error method. These reserved-looking professional women, almost as regimented as soldiers in uniform, roused in him uneasy curiosity and distrust. He hoped quite constantly he was going to meet some gay young girls, students perhaps; there seemed to be plenty of them about, but not one had given him the eye yet. He had stopped in a doorway and hastily jotted a few broad-bottomed figures, sagging faces, and dressed pigs, in his notebook. He sketched a specially haggard and frustrated looking streetwalker with a preposterous tilt to her feathered hat. He tried at first not to be seen at his occupation, but discovered soon that he need not worry, for, in fact, nobody noticed him.

These rather scattered impressions were in his mind and he was very dissatisfied with all of them as he folded up his map and pamphlet and set out walking to find a room in Berlin. In the first dozen squares he counted five more of those rather sick-looking young men with fresh wounds in their cheeks, long heavy slashes badly mended with tape and cotton, and thought again that nobody had told him to expect that.

Two days later he was still tramping the snowy streets, ringing doorbells and crawling back to the little hotel in the evenings pretty well dead on his feet. On the morning of the third day, when his search brought him finally to the third floor of a solid looking apartment house in Bambergerstrasse, he took pains to observe very attentively the face of the woman who opened the door. In such a short time he had learned a wholesome terror of landladies in that city. They were smiling foxes, famished wolves, slovenly house cats, mere tigers, hyenas, furies, harpies: and sometimes worst of all they were sodden melancholy human beings who carried the history of their disasters in their faces, who all but wept when they saw him escape, as if he carried their last hope with him. Except for four winters in a minor southern university, Charles had lived at home. He had never looked for a lodging before, and he felt guilty, as if he had been peeping through cracks and keyholes, spying upon human inadequacy, its kitchen smells and airless bedrooms, the staleness of its poverty and the stuffiness of its prosperity. He had been shown spare cubbyholes back of kitchens where the baby's wash was drying on a string while the desolate room waited for a tenant. He had been ushered into regions of gilded carving and worn plush, full of the smell of yesterday's cabbage. He had ventured into bare expanses of glass brick and chrome-steel sparsely set out with white leather couches and mirror-topped tables, where, it always turned out, he would be expected to stay for a year at least, at frightening expense. He peered into a sodden little den fit, he felt, only for the scene of a murder; and into another where a sullen young woman was packing up, and the whole room reeked of some nasty perfume from her underwear piled upon the bed. She had given him a deliberately dirty smile, and the landlady had said something in a very brutal tone to her. But mostly, there was a stuffy tidiness, a depressing air of constant and unremitting housewifery, a kind of repellent gentility in room after room after room, varying only in the depth of feather bed and lavishness of draperies, and out of them all in turn he fled back to the street and the comparative freedom of the air.

The woman who opened the door presently, he saw, was a fairly agreeable looking person of perhaps fifty years or more—above a certain age they all looked alike to Charles—

with a pinkish face, white hair and very lively light blue eyes. She gave the impression of being dressed up, she had a little high-faluting manner which seemed harmless and she was evidently very pleased to see him. He noticed that the hall was almost empty but highly polished, perhaps here was the perfect compromise between overstuffed plush and a rat trap.

The landlady showed him her best room, the only one unoccupied, she explained. He might be glad to know she had only young gentlemen in the house, three in fact, she hoped he might make a fourth. "I have here," she said with pride, "a young student from the University of Berlin, a young pianist, and a young student from Heidelberg on leave, so you see the company will not be so bad. May I ask your profession?"

"I am a kind of painter," said Charles, hopefully.

"Charming," said the landlady. "We lacked only an artist."

"I hope you will excuse my poor German," said Charles, a little overwhelmed by all the high manner.

"You will learn," said the landlady, smiling graciously as a mother, and added, "I am Viennese, which accounts perhaps for any little difference you may notice between my speech and that which you hear ordinarily in Berlin. I may say, the Viennese way of talking is not the worst in the world, if you really wish to learn German while you are here."

The room. Well, the room. He had seen it several times

before in his search. It was not what he would choose if he had a choice, but it was the least tiresome example of what he recognized now as a fixed style, with its sober rich oriental carpet, the lace curtains under looped-back velvet hangings, the large round table covered with another silky oriental rug in sweet, refined colors. One corner was occupied by deep couches heaped with silk and velvet cushions, the wall above it adorned with a glass-doored cabinet filled with minute curiosities mostly in silver filigree and fine porcelain, and upon the table stood a huge lamp with an ornate pink silk shade, fluted and fringed and draped with silken tassels. The bed was massive with feather quilt and shot-silk cover, the giant wardrobe of dark polished wood was carved all out of shape.

A hell of a place, really, but he would take it. The landlady looked human, and the price was no higher than he would be asked anywhere else for such a monstrosity. She agreed at once that he would need a plain work table and a student lamp, and added, "I hope you expect to stay for six months."

"I'm sorry," said Charles, who had been waiting for this. "Only three months."

The landlady concealed her disappointment unsuccessfully in a sweet little smile. "It is usual to agree for six months," she told him.

"But I am going to another country in three months," said Charles.

"Oh, really? Where are you going?" she asked, and her whole face lighted as if the prospect of travel were her own.

"To Italy, perhaps," said Charles. "First to Rome and then to Florence. And then all over Europe," he added recklessly, feeling certain for the first time that this was really true, it was bound to happen.

"Oh, Italy," cried the landlady. "I spent the three happiest months of my life there, I have dreamed of going back."

Charles was standing near the table. On the silk rug, near the lamp, there stood a small plaster replica, about five inches high, of the Leaning Tower of Pisa. As they talked, his hand wandered towards it, he picked it up lightly by the middle with his finger tips, and the delicate plaster ribs caved in. They simply crumbled at his touch, and the fragments dropped around the weighted base as he snatched back his hand. He saw in horror that the landlady had gone very pale, her blue eyes instantly suffused.

Charles' self-possession crumbled with the tower. He stammered, "Oh, I'm so sorry," seeing that to the landlady the accident was serious and feeling himself shamefully exposed before her in his proved and demonstrated clumsiness, the aimless wandering curiosity of his mind, his bad habit of pawing things. Why couldn't he have kept his hands to himself? "Please allow me to replace it."

"It cannot be replaced," said the landlady, with a severe, stricken dignity. "It was a souvenir of the Italian journey. My husband and I brought it back as a pleasantry from our honeymoon. My husband has been dead for many years. No, the little tower is not a thing that can be replaced."

Charles, wishing to escape with his humiliation into the open air, said, "Perhaps I had better go for my luggage. I will be back in an hour."

"Yes," she said, absently, gathering up the ruins bit by bit on a sheet of paper. "My only hope is, it may be repaired."

"Do please let me pay for that, at least," said Charles. "I am so very sorry."

"It is not your fault, but mine," said the landlady, "I should never have left it here for—" She stopped short, and walked away carrying the paper in her two cupped hands. For barbarians, for outlandish crude persons who have no respect for precious things, her face and voice said all too clearly.

Charles, red and frowning, moved warily around the furniture towards the windows. A bad start, a very bad start indeed. The double panes were closed tightly, the radiator cast an even warmth through the whole room. He drew the lace curtains and saw, in the refracted pallor of the midmorning, winter light, a dozen infant-sized pottery cupids, gross, squat limbed, wanton in posture and vulgarly pink, with scarlet feet and cheeks and backsides, engaged in what appeared to be a perpetual scramble to avoid falling off the steep roof of a house across the street. Charles observed grimly their realistic toe holds among the slate, their clutching fat hands, their imbecile grins. In pouring rain, he thought, they must keep up their senseless play. In snow, their noses would be completely buried. Their behinds were natural victims to the winter winds. And to think that whoever had put them there had meant them to be oh, so whimsical and so amusing, year in, year out. He clutched his hat and overcoat with a wild impulse to slip out quietly and disappear. Maybe he wouldn't come back at all. He hadn't signed or paid anything yet. Oh, yes, but he would, though. For the landlady appeared at once, again smiling and composed, carrying a card, a slip of paper with printing on it, pen, ink, and her receipt blanks, all on a silver tray. He did not escape without leaving on that tray a full report of himself for the benefit of the police, a signed agreement to keep the room for three months, and a month's rent in marks, instead of dollars. "What a pity you have no dollars," she said brightly, and tilted her head at him in a brave gesture of acceptance. On her left hand she wore a rather inordinate diamond, square and blue, obviously a very fine one, set elaborately at great height. He had not noticed it before.

The sallow wornout looking hotel proprietess greeted him with an almost pleasant expression when he approached her desk. He was surprised at the violent change in her face when he explained that he had found another room and would be leaving at once. Instantly she seemed ready to weep with anger and disappointment.

"But I do not understand," she told him stiffly, her lids reddening. "You agree to stay for a month, I give you very special rates, and now in eight days you are saying you must go. Do you find us disagreeable, perhaps? Isn't your room cared for properly? What has happened?"

"It is simply true that I must find something less expensive still," he told her, carefully. "That is all."

"But our charges here are most reasonable," she said, her dry mouth working over her long teeth. "Why will you not stay?"

"They are reasonable," he admitted, feeling cornered, and as if he were making a humiliating confession, "but I cannot afford them."

The woman opened her account book and began copying from it rapidly, her face stiff with indignation as if she had caught him snatching her purse. "That is your own business," she told him, in a low voice, "but naturally you must expect to pay by the day, in this case."

"Naturally," he agreed.

"You will find you cannot change your mind for nothing," said the woman, in a severe, lecturing tone. "Indecision is a very expensive luxury."

"I suppose so," said Charles, uneasily watching the notations on the sheet of paper lengthening rapidly.

She glanced up and over his shoulder, and Charles saw her face change again to a hard boldness, she raised her voice sharply and said with insolence, "You will pay your bill as I present it or I shall call the police."

Charles, who had his money in hand ready to pay what she asked, believed for an instant he had not understood properly. Turning in the direction of her glance, he saw standing a few feet away the middle-aged podgy partner. His head was like a soft block, covered with scanty gray bristles. Hands in pockets he was eyeing Charles with a peculiarly malignant smile on his wide lipless mouth. Charles, amazed at the sum written at the foot of the page, counted out the money to the last pfennig, suddenly afraid that if he gave her a round sum she would not give him back the change. She swept it away from him, together with the bill, without speaking.

"Will you please give me the receipt?" asked Charles.

She did not answer, but moved away a little, and the man approached silently and said in a voice of edged, false courtesy, "I must require you, before you go, to let me see your papers."

Charles said, "I showed them when I came here," and picked up his suitcases.

"But not to me," said the man, and his pale little eyes behind their puffy lids were piggish with malice. "Not to me, I am sorry to say, and that will be necessary before you are allowed to go, let me assure you."

He seemed struggling with some hidden excitement. His neck swelled and flushed, he closed his mouth until it was a mere slit across his face, and rocked slightly on his toes. Charles had been well prepared for the nuisance of being under constant observation, experienced travelers had told him he would feel like a criminal on parole in Europe, especially in Germany, at first, but that he would soon grow accustomed to it, and he was to be certain to hand his papers over at once to anyone who asked for them. He set his suitcases down and felt in his pockets, then remembered he had tucked the flat leather case containing his papers in one of his suitcases. Which one?

He opened the larger of the two, exposing a huddle of untidy clothing. The man and the woman leaned forward to gaze at his belongings, and the woman said, "So," in a contemptuous voice. Charles, in outraged silence, closed the suitcase and opened the other. He handed the leather case to the man, who drew out the passports and other papers one by one with maddening slowness, regarded them with a skeptical eye, puffing his cheeks and clicking his tongue by turns. With deliberation he handed them back and said, "Very good. You may go now," with the insulting condescension of a petty official dismissing a subordinate.

They continued to look at him in a hateful silence, with

their faces almost comically distorted in an effort to convey the full depths of their malice. It was as if they doubted, from his manner, that he had understood the extent to which they were insulting and cheating him, or as if, being safe in their advantage, they wished to goad him to protest so they might do him further damage. Awkardly under their fixed stare, Charles returned his papers to the suitcase, closed it with difficulty after some trouble with the fastenings. As the door closed behind him he heard them laughing together like a pair of hyenas, with deliberate loudness, to make certain he should hear them.

He felt all at once rather too poor to afford a taxicab, so he walked, lugging his rather battered possessions, and as their weight increased and the distance stretched before him, he meditated rather shapelessly on the treatment he had just received. He was a tall, personable young man, there was nothing wrong with his looks or his intentions, though at that moment, a trifle beetle-browed, hat over eyes, he seemed sullen and rather ugly. His first furious impulse to hit the fat man in the teeth with his fist had been overcome instantly by the clear cold spot in his mind which knew that this situation was hopeless, there was no chance for any sort of reparation, he could either keep quiet and escape from the two thugs or quite simply he would be in worse trouble. His anger remained and settled, took root and became a new part of him.

His landlady opened the door for him again. He observed there seemed to be no servant about the place. After a few more formalities of greeting, restlessly he took to the street again, telling himself he needed a haircut. Consulting his map, he bore towards Kurfürstendamm. The sun had disappeared, it was colder suddenly, the snow began to fall again on the smooth dark streets gleaming in the light like polished metal. The weighty laborious city was torpid in the early darkness.

The barber shop was small and clean, wrapped in white towels, shining with mirrors and full of warm soapy steam. A weakly shaped, bloodless little man took him in hand and began to tuck cloths around his neck. He had scanty discouraged hair the color of tow, and a sickly, unpleasant breath. He wanted to cut Charles' hair long on top, clip it to the skin around the back of his head in a wide swath over the ears. His own was cut that way, the streets were full of such heads, and a photograph, clipped from a newspaper and stuck in the corner of the mirror, showed a little shouting politician, top lock on end, wide-stretched mouth adorned by a square mustache, who had, apparently, made the style popular. It required a great deal of head shaking, rather desperately assembled German, some pointing to other photographs in a barber's journal of fashion, to persuade the man to a more reasonable point of view.

The barber, sad enough at his gayest, drooped rather more

as he tapered Charles' hair almost imperceptibly towards the neck; and to change the whole topic he spoke of the weather. The last day or two had been mild, even milder than anyone thought, for it had deceived the storks. The papers that morning had mentioned that storks had been seen flying over the city, certain signs of good weather and an early spring. Had the young gentleman noticed a dispatch from New York that said the trees in Central Park were putting out green buds–imagine, at this time of year.

"There is nothing in the Tiergarten at this time," said the little barber, sighing. "This is a dark place in winter. I lived in Malaga once, I worked there in a barber shop for a whole year–nearly thirteen months, in fact. The barber shops there are not like ours, they are very dirty, but there, flowers were in bloom outside, in December. There, they use real almond oil for their hair lotions–real. And they have such an extract of rosemary as you cannot find anywhere else. Olive oil the poorer people use for their hair, as well as for cookery. Olive oil, imagine, here so expensive, there they pour it out on their heads. Olive oil, they told me, inside and out, that is what makes hair grow. Well, maybe. Here, everyone wants his hair dry, and mostly," he returned to the hateful subject, "they like it close above the ears and full on top. Say it is only our poor German taste," he said sourly, and then, "In Malaga, I never wore my topcoat all winter. Ah, I hardly knew it was winter." His fingers were clammy and his front teeth looked weak, as if they had never got a proper start. "It was strange there in many ways, naturally, considering the kind of people they are, but then they did not have to worry so much about living. Sometimes, there, I put my hand in my pocket and felt my last peseta, but I was not alarmed as I would have been here. I thought that when that was gone I could get more. I should have saved something there," he said, with a guilty look, "but I did not, and here I save and save, but there is nothing." He coughed, turning his head away. "In Malaga," he said, and he was like a man talking about a homeland he had lost, "I never had a cough, though here I cough all the time."

"Flu?" asked Charles, through the towels.

"No, gas," said the little barber, modestly. "The war."

After a dismal pause, Charles said, "I noticed the other day that Malaga froze stiff too, this winter."

"Well, yes, once perhaps, but only for a few days," admitted the barber, shaking his head slowly. "Once, perhaps—"

When Charles felt carefully in his pocket for the smallest coin he could give, uneasy because he knew it was not enough, but all at once unnerved by caution, not daring to reduce his cash store by a single pfennig more than necessary, the barber held out his bluish narrow hand, glanced discreetly into the palm, smiled and said with genuine feeling, "Thank you, thank you very much." Charles nodded his head, in shame, and hurried away.

The knob turned from within and the door flew open as Charles was bending, key in hand, and the landlady fluted at him sweetly. She had been expecting him, she had wondered what was keeping him, she had happened to be in the hall and had heard his step on the stair. She believed she had him nicely settled now, and at what hour would he have his afternoon coffee? Charles said he supposed five o'clock would be all right. "So," she said, smiling and tilting her head at him with what struck Charles as a slightly too intimate, possessive gleam. Still smiling, she hurried away to the farther end of the hall and rapped sharply at a closed door.

It was opened at once, and Charles got a full glimpse of a drooping heavy-set dark young man with a big cropped head and blunt features. The landlady went straight past him, talking in a rapid authoritative tone as if she were giving orders. Charles closed his own door with some relief and looked around for his luggage. It had disappeared. He glanced into the big wardrobe and saw with a peculiar sense of invasion that his things were unpacked—he had long since lost the keys and had never got into the habit of locking things, anyway—and arranged with an orderliness that exposed all their weaknesses of quality and condition. His shoes, needing minor repairs and a coat of polish, were set in wooden supports. His other two suits, the tweed with its buttons hanging, were on silk padded frames. His meager toilet articles, his frayed hair brushes and his flabby leather cases were in array on the middle shelf. Conspicuous among them, looking somehow disreputable, was his quart bottle of brandy, a third empty, and he realized that he had in effect taken to secret drinking during his search for a room. He peered into the lumpy laundry bag hanging on a hook, and shuddered with masculine shame. Its snowy sweet-smelling whiteness concealed his socks that needed darning, his soiled shirts worn too long for economy's sake, and his stringy underwear. On the pillow of his bed, half concealing the long effeminate lace pillow ruffles, lay a pair of neatly folded clean pajamas.

Last effrontery of all, the woman had unpacked his papers and his drawing material and his cardboard folders of unfinished work. Had she looked into them? He hoped she had a good time. A great many of his sketches were not meant for publication. Everything was laid out carefully stacked with a prime regard for neatness and a symmetrical appearance. He had noticed before the strange antagonism of domesticated females for papers. They seemed to look upon papers as an enemy of order, mere dust-catching nuisances. At home he had waged perpetual silent warfare with his mother and the servants about his papers. They wanted to straighten them out, or better, hide them away in the deepest shelves of a closet. Why in God's name couldn't they let his work alone? But they could not, under their curious compulsion; and neither could this woman, that was clear. Consulting his little phrase book, he began constructing and memorizing a polite sentence beginning, "Please don't trouble yourself about my table . . ."

The table was large, though not plain, the lamp was good enough, but the straight-backed chair was a delicate affair with curved spindle legs and old mended tapestry in seat and back: a museum piece beyond doubt, Charles decided, and sat upon it experimentally. It held up. He proposed to overlook and forget the whole damned situation, put his stuff in order and get to work. First he emptied his pockets of accumulated bits of notes, sketches, receipts, scribbled addresses of restaurants, postcard reproductions of paintings he had bought at museums, and the agreement he had signed to stay in this house for three months. He noticed that the landlady's name was Rosa Reichl, written in a tall, looping, affectedly elegant hand. He could not see the end of those three months. He felt a blind resentment all the more deep because it could have no particular object, and helpless as if he had let himself be misled by bad advice. Vaguely but in the most ghastly sort of way, he felt that someone he trusted had left him in the lurch, and of course, that was nonsense, as Kuno used to say. "Nonsense" was one of Kuno's favorite words, especially just after his returns from abroad.

The voices in the next room were going on, rising and tightening somewhat with an excitement that might be anger. Charles listened carefully with no sense of eavesdropping, as always surprised that he understood German so well and spoke it so poorly.

"Herr Bussen, Herr Bussen," Frau Reichl was crying, in a flighty, impassioned voice, her light Viennese accent slightly blurred, "you treat my good chairs like this, my beautiful old chairs I have had for so long—in spite of my other troubles you must add this? How can you, when you know I shall never have chairs like these again?"

Charles, who had begun testing crayons and sharpening pencils, stopped to light a cigarette, leaning back in his own chair. He balanced on the back legs for a split second and came down with a thump, his heart seeming to turn over as the thin joints complained in a human voice.

Herr Bussen, who began by defending himself half-heartedly, gave in and took his scolding dutifully as if Frau Reichl were his mother or his conscience. Yes, he knew better, Charles heard him saying in heavy Low-German, he had been brought up properly even if she did not think so. His mother had such chairs too, he would not let it happen again. Herr Bussen's speech sounded to Charles like some ungainly English dialect, but in no language would he have been a match for Frau Reichl. Charles found himself feeling very sorry for that poor devil as he blundered on apologizing; she was to excuse him this time if she could.

"Yes, this time," rejoined Frau Reichl, exasperated to a point beyond all grace, "this time," she said sarcastically in her sweetest tones, "and how many others, past and to come?"

Herr Bussen found no answer for this. After a silent moment of triumph, Frau Reichl emerged and swished past Charles' door while he waited uneasily for her to stop before it, and knocked on the door just next his at the right.

"*Jawohl!*" shouted the young man inside in the drowning voice of one dredged too suddenly out of sleep. "Yes, yes, come in." Then a gay and youthful voice cleared and added, "Oh, it's you, Rosa dear. Well, I thought there must be a fire."

Rosa, is it? thought Charles, hearing their voices running on together, quick and friendly, in lowered tones, with now and again a small duet of good-humored laughter. Rosa seemed very cheerful indeed, moving about the room as she talked, crossing the hall to her own apartment and back several times. At last she said, "Now then, please tell me when you need anything. Only, no more ice. There is no more."

"Who cares?" called the young man, and Rosa laughed again. Charles began to think of her as Rosa, and a nuisance, if affairs went on at this rate all day in the house.

Daylight had failed. Charles settled himself firmly to his drawing under the lamp which was better than he expected. He began with many small anxieties. Suppose that editor changed his mind? Suppose his drawing were not published and paid for, after all? How long could his father continue to send him money? How long, and this was the real question, this was what worried him most, how long should he go on taking money from his father? Should he have come to Europe at all? A lot of good painters had never been in Europe. He tried to think of one. Well, he was here, horribly disturbed and miserable really, he might as well face it, he had got a much harder blow than he expected from the place. At least he must try to find what he came for, if it wasn't to be just a wild goose chase. He refused to listen any further to the sounds in the house, but focused his eyes upon a certain spot on the paper, remembered what he meant to do, and went to work. All his energy seemed to flow and balance in his right hand, he felt steadied and at ease, he belonged to himself and knew what he was doing. Then he forgot himself altogether. Some time later he sat back and looked at what he had done. It wouldn't do, it was absolutely all wrong.

A light rap on the door saved him. He had an excuse to stop, to turn the page over and let it cool off before he looked at it again. Hardly waiting for his word, Rosa came in. She glanced sharply first at the light and then at the table, already in disorder.

"Ah, you need light early, I see," she commented, with an uncertain smile, a deprecating tilt of the head. "As for Herr Bussen, he does not work in the evenings until after supper. And Herr Mey, the Polish gentleman, quite often plays in the dark because he wishes. Our young student from Heidelberg doesn't have anything to think about but his face at this moment, and the less light on that, the better. Ah me, it is a sight. But," she said, fondly and mysteriously, "he is young, it is his first, he will know what to expect the next time. But the wound is infected, you know, he is here for treatment. Ah, the young one," she said, tenderly, clasping her hands over her breast, "he is very brave all day, but when the dark comes, it is very hard for him. He is so young and tender," she told Charles, almost tearful in her pride and pity, "but he did well, you can see. The wound—well, it is a beauty!"

She moved about the room while she talked, straightening the chairs ever so little, giving a flick at the cushions here, a whisk at the curtains there. Standing beside Charles at the table, she even reached round him to take a light turn among his papers, setting up a small commotion by moving his ash tray and the India ink a few inches out of their places. "After all, there is no more daylight," she admitted, finally, "and if you draw, you need light, isn't it true? Now I shall bring your coffee at once," she promised, brightly, and went away with that extraordinarily busy air of hers.

No more daylight. Charles, feeling helpless, as if he were taking part in a play, and had forgotten his lines if he ever knew them, watched the street as he waited, silent under the falling snow, empty in the frosty shimmer of the corner lamps. Lights were coming on one by one in the many windows of the houses opposite.

In the past few days he had watched each morning by lamplight the feeble sun crawl later and later barely to the level of the housetops, slide slowly around in a shallow arc and drop away in midafternoon. The long nights oppressed him with unreasonable premonitions of danger. The darkness closed over the strange city like the great fist of an enemy who had survived in full strength, a voiceless monster from a prehuman, older and colder and grimmer time of the world. "It is just because I was born in a sunny place and took the summer for granted," he told himself, but that did not explain why he could not endure with patience, even enjoy, even look upon as something new and memorable to see, unfamiliar weather in a foreign climate. Of course it was not the weather. No one paid attention to weather if he had the proper clothes for it; he rememberd a teacher of his saying once that all great cities are built in uninhabitable places. He knew that people love even the worst of the climate in the place they know, and can wonder at the feelings of strangers about it. At home in Texas he had seen northern travelers turn upon the southern weather with the ferocity of exhaustion; it gave them the excuse they needed to hate everything else they hated in the place, too. It would be so easy and simple, it would put such an end to the argument to be able to say, "I can't settle down in this place because the sun doesn't rise until ten o'clock in December," but that was not his trouble here.

There were the faces. Faces with no eyes. And these no-eyes, pale, lightless, were set in faces shriveled as if they were gnawed hollow; or worse, faces sodden in fat with swollen eyelids in which the little no-eyes peered blindly as if all the food, the plates of boiled potatoes and pig's knuckles and cabbage fed to the wallowing body, had weighed it down and had done it no good. The no-eyes in the faces of the women were too ready to shed tears. Charles had not understood in the least the first thing that had happened to him in Berlin. He had bought some cheap socks in a little shop. At the hotel he saw they were too small, and had gone back at once to exchange them for a larger size. The woman who had sold them to him saw him coming in with the package in his hand, had remembered him and instantly stood transfixed, the tears welling up in her eyes. While he was trying to explain in awful embarrassment that he merely wished larger socks in place of those she had given him, the tears rolled over her cheeks and she said, "I have no larger size."

"Could you get them for me?" he asked, and she said, "Oh, yes," in such pain that Charles said awkwardly, "Don't bother, I'll keep these," and ran out, annoyed and mystified. A day or two later it was all clear to him and seemed quite natural. She needed badly to sell the stock she had. She could not afford to order just a few pairs of larger socks. She was frightened at seeing the goods she had on hand, unsold, and she had deliberately given him the socks she had already, hoping he could not, a stranger, a traveler, find his way back to complain.

Men who sold wine and fruit in tiny corners did not seem to prosper in their rich and warming commodities, they got no nourishment of their company and obviously they could not afford to enjoy them. These men were silent, usually middle-aged, deeply sullen, and if Charles asked them a question, hearing the foreign voice they would shout out their answer as if in a burst of fury, though the words were harmless. Among themselves they talked in a dead tone of disheartenment that seemed an old habit. With his limited money, he was frightened to go to any place where things were for sale. Because he was poor, he went to poor places, and felt trapped, for they could not let him go until he had bought something. They tried desperately to sell him things he did not want or need, could not use, or could not afford. It was no good trying to explain this to them. They could not hear him.

No more daylight. No more ice. No more chairs with tapestry on them and legs that broke if you leaned back in them. No more of those table rugs with their nasty sweet colors. If the corner whatnot should be knocked over, just once, there would be no more of that silly bric-a-brac and a good thing too, thought Charles, hardening his heart.

"Coffee at last," said Rosa, coming in without knocking this time, carrying a very dressed up tray. No more coffee at five o'clock, unless you were a foreigner, and–it followed naturally–rich. Charles felt he was living under false pretenses of the kind his early training had taught him to despise. "I am poorer than she is," he thought, watching Rosa arrange the fine porcelain cup with butterfly handle, and spread out thin napery. "But of course not. A boat is coming from America for me, but there is no boat for her. For nobody in this house but me is a boat coming from America, with money. I can get along here, I can leave when I like, I can always go home–"

He felt young, ignorant, awkward, he had so much to learn he hardly knew where to begin. He could always go home, but that was not the point. It was a long way home from where he stood, he could see that. No more Leaning Tower of Pisa, he remembered with guilt, when Rosa, with a last little fussy pat as if she could not quite give up her coffee table, stood back and said, "Now, if you will sit, I will pour your coffee. Pity it is we are not in Vienna," she told him, with a gay little air, "then I could give you real coffee. But this is not the worst in the world, either." Then she ran away, and the flurry of her wake did not settle until some seconds after she was gone.

The coffee was indeed as good as Charles had ever tasted, more than good enough, and he had just taken the first swallow when he heard Herr Bussen's voice in the hall. "Ha," he pronounced in his loud Low-German, "how that coffee stinks."

"Don't tell me you wouldn't like it just the same," said Rosa cruelly. "Just because you drink milk like a big baby and leave the dirty bottles under the bed. Shame on you, Herr Bussen."

They were silenced in the sound of a piano, struck firmly and softly at first, and then without pause there followed a long rippling continuous music. Charles loved music without knowing how or why, and he listened carefully. That would be the Polish student, and it seemed to Charles he was doing pretty well. He sat back in a pleasant daze, hypnotized by the steady rhythm and delighted with the running melody that he could follow easily. Rosa tapped and came in on tiptoe, finger on lip, eyebrows raised, eyes shining. She approached the table and with careful lightness gathered up the napery and silver. "Herr Mey," she whispered, and then, reverently, "Chopin—" and before Charles could think of any response, she had the tray up and had tiptoed out again.

Charles, lightly asleep, dreamed the house was burning down, silently alive and pulsing with flame in every part. With no fear or hesitation at all, he walked safely through the fiery walls and out into the wide bright street, carrying a suitcase which knocked against his knees and weighed him down, but he could not leave it because it contained all the drawings he meant to do in his whole life. He walked a safe distance and watched the dark skeleton of the house tall as a tower standing in a fountain of fire. Seeing that he was alone, he said in wonder, "They all escaped, too," when a loud and ghostly groan was uttered in his ear. He spun about and saw no one. The groan sounded again over his shoulder and woke him sharply. He found he was wallowing in the airless deeps of the feather quilt, hot and half smothered. He fought his way out and sat up to listen, turning this way and that to locate the sound.

"Ah,–ahooooooo," sighed a voice hopelessly from the room to the right, falling and dying away in a heavily expelled breath of weariness. Without deciding to do anything, Charles found himself at the right hand door tapping with the extreme tips of his fingers.

"Well, what is it?" came a drowsed but soberly indignant voice.

"Is there anything I can do for you?" asked Charles.

"No, no," said the voice in despair. "No, thank you, no no . . ."

"I'm sorry," said Charles, thinking he had been saying this to somebody or other, or thinking it, or feeling it, all day and every day since he had been in that city. The soles of his feet were tingling on the bare floor.

"But come in, please," said the voice, changing to a shade of affability.

The young man sitting on the side of the tumbled bed was of the extreme pale blondness such as Charles had often noticed among the young people in the streets. His hair, eyebrows and eyelashes were pale taffy color, the skin taffy blond, the eyes a flat grayish blue almost expressionless except for a certain modeling of the outer lids that gave him the look of a young, intelligent fox. He had a long, narrow head, with smooth, sharply cut features of the kind Charles vaguely regarded as aristocratic. So far, a good-looking fellow, perhaps twenty-one years old; he stood up slowly and was eye level with Charles' six feet of height. There was only one thing wrong with him: the left side of his face was swollen badly, the eye was almost closed from beneath, and glued along his cheek from ear to mouth was an inch-wide strip of court plaster, the flesh at its edges stained in dirty blues and greens and purples. He was the Heidelberg student, all right. He stood cupping his hand lightly over his cheek without touching.

"Well," he said, keeping his mouth stiff and looking from under his downy light brows at Charles. "You can see for yourself. Nothing to speak of, but it gives me the devil. Like a toothache, you know. I heard myself roaring in my sleep," he said, and his eyes quietly dared Charles to doubt his word. "I woke myself up at it. When you knocked, to tell you the truth, I thought it was Rosa with an ice cap. I don't want any more ice caps. Sit down, please."

Charles said, "I've got some brandy, maybe that would do something."

The boy said, "God, yes," and sighed again in spite of himself. He moved around the room aimlessly, holding his spread hand just beside his face as if he expected his head to drop and hoped to catch it as it fell. His pale gray cotton pajamas gave him the look of being about to fade away in the yellowish light of the bed lamp.

Charles, in his old blanket robe and felt slippers, brought two glasses and the brandy bottle. As he poured, the young man watched the liquid filling the glass as if he would spring upon it, but he held his hands until the glass was offered, smelled the brim, they touched glasses and drank.

"Ah," said the young man, swallowing carefully, head back and tipped to the right. He curled up the right side of his mouth at Charles and his right eye glimmered at him gratefully. "What a relief." He added suddenly, "Hans von Gehring, at your service."

Charles spoke his own name, the other nodded, there was a pause while the glasses were filled again.

"And how do you like it, here in Berlin?" Hans asked politely, warming the brandy between his palms.

"So far, very well," said Charles; "of course, I'm not settled yet." He observed Hans' face in the hope that language was not going to get in the way of their talk. Hans seemed to understand perfectly. He nodded, and drank.

"I've walked nearly all over, and have been to a lot of museums, cafés, all the first things, of course. It is a great city. The Berliners are not proud of it, though, or pretend not to be."

"They know it's no good compared with any other city at all," said Hans, forthrightly. "I was wondering why you came here. Why this city, of all places? You may go where you please, isn't that so?"

"I suppose so," said Charles. "Yes, that's true."

Hans said, "My father sent me here to see a doctor who is an old friend of his, but in ten days I shall be back in Heidelberg. The Polish fellow is a pianist so he came here because pianists seem to think old Schwartzkopf is the only Master. Herr Bussen, down the hall, he is Blatt Deutsch to begin with and he lives in Dalmatia, so anything would perhaps be a change for the better to him. He thinks he is getting an education here and maybe he is. But look at you. A free man and you come to Berlin." He smiled on one side of his face, then shuddered bitterly. "Are you staying on, then?"

"Three months," said Charles, rather gloomily. "I don't know why I came, except that I had a good friend who was

German. He used to come here with his family—that was years ago—and he would say, Go to Berlin. I always thought it was the place to be, and if you haven't seen anything else much, this looks pretty good. Of course, there is New York. I stayed there only about a week, but I liked it, I think I could live there."

"Of course, New York," said Hans, indifferently. "But here, there are Vienna, and Prague, and Munich and Budapest, and Nice and Rome and Florence, and, ah, Paris, Paris, Paris," said Hans, suddenly almost gay. Imitating a German actor imitating a Frenchman, he kissed his fingers and wiggled them lightly towards the west.

"I am going to Paris later," said Charles. "Were you ever there?"

"No, but I am going," said Hans. "My plans are all made." He got up as if his words excited him, wrapped his robe around his knees, felt his cheek tenderly and sat down again.

"I hope to stay there a year, I'm going to some atelier and get some painting done. Maybe you will be there before I leave."

"Oh, I have another year in Heidelberg," said Hans, "and my grandfather, who is old, is giving me the money, so I must stop with him for at least a few months first. But then I may go, I shall be free then for a while, perhaps for two years."

"It is strange to have everything mapped out so," said Charles. "I haven't a notion where I'll be two years from now. Something might even happen to keep me from Paris."

"Oh, it is necessary to plan everything," said Hans, soberly, "or how should we know where we were? Besides, the family has it arranged. I even know the girl I am to marry," he said, "and I know how much money she has. She is an extremely fine girl," he said, without enthusiasm. "Paris will be my own, though, my holiday. I shall do as I please."

"Well," said Charles, seriously, "I am glad to be here. All Americans want to come to Europe one time or another, you know. They think there is something here." He sat back and crossed his legs, feeling comfortable with Hans.

"There is something in Europe," said Hans, "but not in Berlin. You are wasting your time here. Go to Paris if you can." He kicked off his slippers and slid into bed, piling up his pillows and letting his head down very carefully.

"I hope you are feeling better," said Charles. "Perhaps you could sleep now."

Hans frowned slightly, retreated. "There is nothing wrong with me," he declared, "and I was asleep before. This is perfectly normal, it happens quite often."

"Well, good night," said Charles, getting up.

"Oh, no, don't go yet," said Hans, starting to sit up and thinking better of it. "I tell you–knock on Tadeusz' door and get him up, too. He sleeps too much. It's just there, next door. If you please, dear fellow. He'll like it."

A moment of complete silence followed Charles' knock, and in silence the door opened on darkness. A thin, tallish young man, his small sharp head thrust forward like a bird's, appeared in the hall. He wore a thin plum-colored silk dressing gown and his long yellowed hands were flattened one above the other over his chest, the fingers lying together. He seemed entirely awake, and his keen little dark eyes were smiling and good tempered. "What's up now?" he asked in an English accent lying over a Polish accent. "Is the damnation dueler raising hell again?"

"Not exactly," said Charles, pleased at hearing English and astonished at the speech, "but he isn't resting easy, either. We were having some brandy. I'm Charles Upton."

"Tadeusz Mey," said the Pole, sliding out and closing the door noiselessly. He spoke just above a whisper in an easy voice. "Polish in spite of the misleading name. Indiscreet grandmother married an Austrian. The rest of my family have names like Zamoisky, lucky devils."

They entered Hans' room and Tadeusz said instantly in German, "Yes, yes, you are going to have a real beauty," and leaned over to examine the wound with a knowing eye. "It's doing very well."

"It will last," said Hans. Over his face spread an expression very puzzling to Charles. It was there like a change of light, slow and deep, with no perceptible movement of eyelids or face muscles. It rose from within in the mysterious place where Hans really lived, and it was amazing arrogance, pleasure, inexpressible vanity and self-satisfaction. He lay entirely motionless and this look came, grew, faded and disappeared on the tidal movement of his true character. Charles thought, Why, if I drew him without that look I should never have him at all. Tadeusz was talking along in his low voice, amiably in a mixture of French and German. The easy use of languages was a mystery to Charles. He listened acutely, but Tadeusz, gesturing neatly with his brandy glass, did not seem to be saying anything in particular, though Hans was also listening attentively.

Charles, feeling free not to talk, was trying to see Hans in Paris, with that scar. Trying to see him in America, in a small American town like San Antonio, for example, with that scar. In Paris perhaps they would understand, but how would it look in San Antonio, Texas? The people there would think he had got into a disgraceful cutting scrape, probably with a Mexican, or that he had been in an automobile accident. They would think it a pity that such a nice fellow should be so disfigured, they would be tactful and not mention it and try to keep their eyes off it. Even in Paris, Charles imagined, those who understood would also disapprove. Hans would simply be another of those Germans with a dueling scar carefully made livid and jagged to last him a lifetime. It occurred to him that nowhere but in this one small country could Hans boast of his scar and his way of getting it. In any other place at all, it would seem strange, a misfortune, or discreditable. Listening to Tadeusz chattering along, Charles watched Hans and thought hard in a series of unsatisfactory circles, trying to get out of them. It was just a custom of the country, that was all. That was the way to look at it, of course. But Charles didn't know, had never known, very likely never would know, a friend in the world who, if he saw Hans, wouldn't ask privately afterwards, "Where did he get that scar?" Except Kuno, perhaps. But Kuno had never said a word about this. Kuno had said, that if you didn't get off the sidewalk when army officers came along, you would be pushed off, and when his mother and he were walking together, she would always step into the street and let them by. Kuno had not minded this, he had rather admired the tall officers with their greatcoats and helmets, but his mother had not liked it at all. Charles remembered this for years; it was nothing related to anything he knew in his own life, yet remained in his memory as unquestioned truth, that part of Kuno's life lived in absence and strangeness which seemed to him more real than any life they had shared.

Prize fighters got cauliflower ears, but not purposely. It was a hazard of the game. Waiters got something called kidney feet. Glass blowers blow their cheeks all out of shape, so they hang like bags. Violinists sometimes get abscesses on their jaws where they hold the violin. Soldiers now and then have their faces blown off and have to get them put back by surgery. All kinds of things happen to men in the course of their jobs, accidents or just deformities that come on so gradually they are hardly noticed until it is too late to do much about it. Dueling had been a respectable old custom almost everywhere, but there had to be a quarrel first. He had seen his great-grandfather's dueling pistols, the family pride in a velvet-lined case. But what *kind* of man would stand up in cold blood and let another man split his face to the teeth just for the hell of it? And then ever after to wear the wound with that look of self-satisfaction, with everybody knowing how he had got it? And you were supposed to admire him for that. Charles had liked Hans on sight, but there was something he wouldn't know about him if they both lived for a thousand years; it was something you were, or were not, and Charles rejected that wound, the reason why it existed, and everything that made it possible, then and there, simply because there were no conditions for acceptance in his mind.

Still he liked Hans, and wished the wound were not there. But it was there, an improbable and blood-chilling sight, as if at broad noon he should meet in Kurfürstendamm a knight in armor, or the very skeleton from the Dance of Death.

"You don't speak French?" Tadeusz asked at last, turning to Charles.

"A little," said Charles, but fearing to begin.

"You are lucky," said Tadeusz. "You have a language everyone tries to learn. So have the French. But for me, I have to learn every pest of language there is, because no one but a Pole speaks Polish."

He was a narrow, green-faced young man and in the light his eyes were liver colored. He looked bilious, somehow, and he continually twisted a scorched looking lock of hair on the crown of his head as he talked, a tight clever little smile in the corners of his mouth. "I can even speak Blatt Deutsch, but Herr Bussen pretends not to understand me."

"That is the fellow our landlady was scolding today," said Charles, and felt instantly that he had been tactless.

"Today?" asked Tadeusz. "She scolds him every day for one thing or another. He's very stupid. All the Blatt Deutsch are stupid beyond hope. Let Rosa take it all out of him. She won't annoy the rest of us so much. She is a terror, that woman."

"Well," said Hans fretfully, pouting under his lip, "what do you expect? This is a *pension*."

"On the recommended list, too," said Tadeusz, amiably, smoking, holding his cigarette at the base of his third and fourth finger, lighted end towards the palm. "I don't expect anything."

"It would be all right if only she would let my papers alone," said Charles.

"You're the rich American who pays the rent for all of

us," said Tadeusz, smiling. "You've got the real lace curtains and the best feather bed. But if you do anything tactless, remember, Herr Bussen will catch it."

Charles shook his head at this, thinking it was too near the truth to be funny for him, at least. He poured more brandy, and they lighted fresh cigarettes all around. The visitors sat back comfortably and Hans turned on his side. They all felt well disposed and at peace and as if they were beginning to get acquainted with each other. Three sharp little raps upon the door were followed by Rosa's voice. With sweet severity she reminded them in a set speech that it was three o'clock and others in the house might like some sleep. They glanced at each other with conspiratorial smiles.

"Rosa, dear," said Hans, putting a good deal of patient persuasion in his tone, "I was feeling frightfully and they came to sit up with me."

"You do not need anyone to sit up with you," said Rosa, briskly. "You need sleep."

Tadeusz, rising in silence, opened the door suddenly and Rosa fled with small squeaks, an apparition in dressing gown and hair net. He called after her soothingly, "We are going at once," and turned back with a monkeyish gleam in his nearsighted little eyes. "I thought that would rout her," he said, "that woman is vain as if she were twenty. You'd think we were living in a damnation jail," he went on, taking his glass again, "but all Berlin is just that. Let me tell you," he said to Charles, "I can hardly wait to get back to London. You should go there by all means. Believe me, I have seen nearly all the cities—except your fabulous New York, and those photographs made from the air terrorize me—and London is the only place for a civilized man."

Hans shook his head cautiously and repeated, "No, Paris, Paris."

"All right," said Tadeusz in English. "Okay. I learned that from one of your Americans: typical 100 per cent specimen, he told me. He was a cowboy from Arizona with a five gallon hat. He was a Holy Roller and a vegetarian and he drank a tumblerful of whiskey every morning before breakfast. He was in love with a snake charmer who also did a fan dance. When I knew him he was running a little *boîte* on the Left Bank; the walls were covered with steer's horns and lariats. When he quarreled with the snake charmer, he dragged her all around the floor by one of the lariats. She left him at once, but not before putting a venomous serpent in his bed. However, no harm was done. As he said, it was all okay by him."

Hans said, "What are you saying, please? Remember I don't know English."

Tadeusz said in German, "I was explaining where I learned to say Okay."

Hans nodded. "Ah, yes, I understand that very well, okay. That is the only English I know."

By way of proving they were still men, masters of themselves, they lingered somewhat and took their sweet time about saying good night and separating.

Charles, emerging from the bathroom in the morning, met Herr Bussen in the hall. Herr Bussen was wearing a short cotton bathrobe and carrying a rather draggled towel. His fat round face wore a grieved and bewildered look, like a child who had been so sternly treated at home it did not expect better from the rest of the world. Charles had been wakened by the sound of Rosa scolding Herr Bussen about something or other. Presently she came in with coffee and rolls and butter, looking very well combed and dressed so early in the morning, but with a light sparkle of roused temper in her eyes. She opened the curtains and turned out the light, leaving the winter day like dirty water in the room. She spun away and knocked at the bathroom door, saying in a prissy voice of authority, "It is fifteen minutes, your time is up, Herr Bussen." Returning, she stripped the bed with one gesture, creating a small breeze over Charles' head as he sat at the table. Standing close beside him she sighed suddenly: "Oh, how hard it is to have an orderly and peaceful life, a correct life of the kind I was accustomed to. And the bathroom. Always shaving soap, toothpaste and water, water on the linoleum, the mirrors themselves splashed, everything so unclean, oh, Herr Upton, I do not know why gentlemen will never wash the bathtub. And oh, the Herr Bussen. Every day his bed is full of cheese and bread crumbs, there are often tins of sardines open in the chest among his clothes, he eats walnuts and hides the shells in the closet. It is no excuse to say he is going to be a professor. And every month late, late with the rent. How does he think I shall exist if I cannot have the rent promptly?"

Charles, positively blushing all over, got up and said, "If you will wait a few minutes, I am going out and won't trouble you."

"Ah, you don't trouble me. I am going about my work, you about yours. No, it is not that." She smiled brightly upon him, her despair seemed to pass. "Let me tell you, before the war I had five servants besides a gardener and a chauffeur, my frocks came from Paris and my furniture from England; I had three diamond necklaces, Herr Upton, three —so now, is it strange that sometimes I wonder what is to become of me? I make up beds like a servant," she said, "and I wash dirty floors. . . ."

Charles, feeling cornered, got his hat and coat, stammered a sentence in German unintelligible to himself even, and rushed away, appalled at Rosa's lack of decency in her confidences, and her shameful knowledge of his own untidy bathroom habits.

He pawned his camera, expecting to get almost nothing for it, but the quiet little man in the shop took his thin nose out of a book, examined the handsome contrivance with professional approval, and gave him a hundred marks without question. Feeling unreasonably rich and cheered up, Charles rushed back to the apartment hoping to work for a while. A few steps from his own door, he saw Herr Bussen going in, clutching a small brown paper parcel—bread and liver sausage, perhaps—and without an overcoat in the wolfish cold. Charles overtook him on the stairway, for Herr Bussen was moving slowly, his shoulders bent. From the back he appeared to be a middle-aged man, but the face he turned to Charles seemed even younger than it should have been, with an underlying half-spent childhood still lingering in it. His nose was red and wet, his eyes were full of tears, his bare hand holding the parcel was cracked at the knuckles.

"Good morning," said Herr Bussen, and his lumpy face lightened, just for a moment, as if he expected something pleasant to happen. Charles slowed down, they exchanged names, and went on together in silence. Rosa opened the door for them.

"Ah," she remarked, glancing from one to the other suspiciously, "so you are acquainted already?"

"Yes," they said in one voice, and strong in solidarity, they moved past her without another word. Rosa disappeared into her own part of the house, talking to herself.

"Does she insult you every time she speaks to you?" asked Herr Bussen, with resigned patience.

"Not yet," said Charles, who was beginning to find his immunity a disadvantage. He felt he was on the wrong side, he would not if he could help it be a pet of Rosa's. Herr Bussen said, "Every day she insults me for at least half an hour, then she goes and insults Herr Mey, but in a different way, for he is very sharp and answers her in little ways she does not understand, but he really insults her in turn. She makes a house cat of Herr von Gehring because he fought a *mensur*, but it won't last, and she is polite to you because you are a foreigner and pay more rent than we do. But you wait. Your turn will come."

"Well, when it does," said Charles, easily, "I'll just get out."

"And pay your whole three months' rent or have her report you to the police?" asked Herr Bussen in wonder. "My God, you *must* be rich."

Charles shook his head, feeling that it was all pretty much no use. A look of envy so deep it was almost hatred spread over Herr Bussen's face, he paused and his eye wandered over Charles from head to foot as if he were some improbable faintly repellant creature of another species. "Ah, well," he said, "seriously, I advise you to observe our curious customs, and do nothing, not the smallest thing, to attract the attention of the police. I tell you this because you are unfamiliar with the country—they are not fond of outlanders here."

"Thank you," said Charles stuffily, feeling deeply offended.

This melancholy conversation first depressed him, then it put him in a temper. He sat down in a dull but pleasant fury and began to draw hastily, without plan. Now and then he raised his elbows, drew his lungs full of air. The walls seemed to be closing in upon him, he imagined he could hear the breathing of those people in the other rooms, he smelt the iodoform on Hans' bandage, the spoiled sardines on Herr Bussen's breath, Rosa's sweetish female hysteria made him ill. He drew the people at the hotel, the woman a sick fox, the man half pig, half tiger. He drew Herr Bussen's unenlightened face, several times, growing more tender with each version. There was something about the fellow. With concentrated malice he drew Rosa, first as kitchen sloven, then as a withered old whore, finally without any clothes on. Studying these, he decided he had paid off a large installment of his irritation with her, and tore them all into minute bits. Instantly he regretted it, but there was no place to hide them from her. Then quite calmly he began to draw Hans' face from the memory of that strange expression of pride in his wound, and this absorbed him so that he grew calm, was ashamed of his anger, wondered what had got into him. They were all good people, they were in terrible trouble, jammed up together in this little flat with not enough air or space or money, not enough of anything, no place to go, nothing to do but gnaw each other. I can always go home, he told himself, but why did I come here in the first place?

The sound of Tadeusz' piano stopped him. He listened with pleasure, sitting back at ease. That fellow really could play. Charles had heard a great many famous pianists, by radio, who didn't, it seemed to him, sound so much better than that. Tadeusz knew what he was doing. He drew Tadeusz sitting over the piano, bird head, little stiff wrinkles at the corners of his mouth, fingers like bird claws. "Hell, maybe I'm a caricaturist," he thought, but he did not really worry about it. He settled down again and forgot to listen.

A scurrying about in the hall and Rosa's voice raised in a shrill whimpering got through to him slowly, he did not wake up altogether until she was beating at his door, crying aloud in real terror, "Oh, God, oh, God, Herr Upton, come and help me. Come help. Herr Bussen–" Charles opened the door. Tadeusz and Hans were already at Herr Bussen's door. Rosa's face was streaming with tears, her hair was draggled. "Herr Bussen has poisoned himself."

Charles shuddered with a mortal chill of fear. He came straight out and joined the others and they went in to Herr Bussen's room together.

Herr Bussen was kneeling beside his bed, clutching a large bedroom jar in his arms, vomiting and retching, speechless except for a gasp between convulsions. Yet he could still raise his hand in a violent waving motion, gurgling, "Go away, go away. . . ."

"Get him to the bathroom," cried Rosa, "fetch a doctor, bring water, for God's sake look out for the rug," and while Charles seized Herr Bussen under the arms to lift him up, Tadeusz came with wet towels and Hans, holding his face, ran to the telephone.

"No, no, God damn it," shouted Herr Bussen, fiercely. "No doctor, no." Freeing himself partially from Charles, he doubled up over the footboard of his bed, holding his stomach, apparently in his agony, his face a terrifying purple green, a shower of sweat pouring over his eyebrows and nose.

"Oh, why did you do it?" cried Rosa, weeping. "To poison yourself, here among your friends, how could you?"

Herr Bussen collected himself for protest. "I tell you, I did not poison myself," he shouted in a good strong baritone, "I told you, I ate something and it poisoned me." He collapsed again over the jar, and the upheavals recommenced.

"Get him to the bathroom," cried Rosa, wringing her hands. "I know," she said, turning on Herr Bussen, indignant again. "That sausage. All those sardines. That liver paste. I warned you, but no, you would not listen. No, you knew best. How many times did I tell you . . ."

"Let me alone," cried Herr Bussen, desperately. "Leave me."

Charles and Tadeusz joined forces. "Come on," said Tadeusz, in Blatt Deutsch, with a conversational tone, "come on, we'll help you."

They took hold of him around the middle so that he hung down rather like a sack, and began hauling him as well as they could. "Oh, Almighty God," groaned Herr Bussen in sincere despair, "let me alone." But they got him in the bathroom, with no more regard for his feelings than if he were already dead, closed the door and locked it. At once Charles came out again, and left the apartment at a run, without his hat. He was back in a very few minutes with a large package, purchases from a pharmacy, and again closing the bathroom door, ignoring Rosa's questions, he and Tadeusz got to work on Herr Bussen seriously.

Rosa turned on Hans, her face quite sodden by then, and still weeping, ordered him back to bed. Hans said, "No, don't trouble yourself. I am better, I am going out to the clinic now."

"You will make yourself worse," wept Rosa.

"No, you may be surprised, I shall be quite all right," said Hans, coolly, leaving.

Herr Bussen, eased, soothed, cleansed, safe in bed with an ice cap on his brow, the object of all attention from his three new friends, lay in bitter, ungrateful silence. He does not seem to be very pleased with us, thought Charles, and we did a roaring good job, too. Herr Bussen—why did they call him that? He wasn't more than twenty-four years old—seemed sunken and shame-faced, he kept his eyes closed or turned to the wall, and when Tadeusz came in with hot soup from a restaurant, he shook his head and seemed about to shed tears. Rosa was injured by the sight of the soup, also.

"You must let me prepare his food," she said to Tadeusz, "I do not want him poisoned again." She took away the soup and brought it again freshly hot on an elegant tray. She seemed very subdued and Herr Bussen was melancholy and without appetite.

Charles, noticing the piles of papers on Herr Bussen's desk, saw written upon them only endless mathematical calculations which he could recognize but not read. Rosa fidgeted among them, trying to straighten them out. In the hall she said to Charles, "You may not know it, but Herr Bussen is considered, at the University, to be a very brilliant mathematician. He promises to become a very learned man." She spoke with pride and possessiveness. "If I am annoyed with him at times, it is because he needs someone to teach him good habits. He eats—ah, it is no better than offal. And now he is ashamed because you know—you have found him out in his misery. It is a terrible thing to be poor," she said, and the tears seemed to come not only from her eyes but from her skin, the tears and the sweat mingled in a stream and covered her face. "What shall we do? What is to become of us?"

Tadeusz came out and took her by the arm. "Enough of that, Rosa," he said, shaking her gently. "Now what happened, really? Herr Bussen eats a sardine and makes a nuisance of himself. Go and lie down, we will look after him and not disturb anything."

"I am very nervous," said Rosa, smiling at him gratefully.

They looked in upon Herr Bussen. He was lying with his arm thrown over his face, quietly, as if the sleeping powders were taking effect. "Come along with me," said Tadeusz to Charles, "I have an odd spot of brandy, too."

Hans came in with his face done up in fresh lint and court plaster, much improved. He refused brandy and said, "Do you suppose we ought to watch him? Do you suppose?"

"No, I don't believe it for a minute," said Tadeusz, after a small pause. "Do you?" he asked Charles.

"I think he told the truth," said Charles.

"Good," said Hans. "Have one for me," he said, and closed his door.

Tadeusz' narrow room was crowded with an upright piano, and a small silent keyboard which Charles examined, touching stiffly. "I work on that seven hours a day," said Tadeusz, spreading his hands and turning them about, "and you'd better be grateful. Now the damnation suicide is asleep, I shan't be able to play any more today. We may as well get drunk," he said, showing four inches of brandy in a bottle. "Seriously, I don't drink. But if I stayed too long in this place I would."

Charles said, "It's getting me down, too, and I wish I knew why. Compared to really poor people, people I have seen, here and at home, even Herr Bussen is almost rich. Compared to even well-off people, I suppose I'm almost a pauper. But I never felt poor, I never was afraid of it. I always thought that if I really wanted money more than anything else, I could get it. But here–I don't know . . . everybody seems so *crowded*, somehow, so worried, and they can't get their minds off of money for a second."

"They lost that war, please don't forget," said Tadeusz, running his fingers over the silent keyboard that gave forth an even wooden clatter. "That damages a nation's personality no end, you know. But I have no sympathy for them, none. And as for feeling crowded, ha, you would have to be a Pole to know what that means. These big fat ugly people," he said, and he crossed his knees and began torturing his scalp lock. "By God they should be Poles for a while to know what it is to be hungry."

"They aren't all ugly," said Charles. "Not by a long shot."

"Okay," said Tadeusz, indifferently and his little eyes closed. Charles thought, Well, what should I say? Am I supposed to go into an impassioned defense of the Poles? Or a denunciation of the Germans? He was thinking really of his fleece-lined coat, wondering if it would be good enough to offer to Herr Bussen and how to go about it. Could he just knock at his door and say, "Here is a coat I don't happen to need?" Or (no, this wouldn't do), "If you don't have a coat with you, why not use this one for a while?" There should be some way of doing it decently. He explained to Tadeusz and asked for advice.

"Oh, never," said Tadeusz. "You can't do that. He is very proud and he would be furious as hell. And besides," Tadeusz swung a foot, "we have to realize that a man's sufferings are his own, quite often he chooses them to some ends of his own—how do we know? We pity people too often for the wrong reasons. They may not need it or want it at all, you know. Poor Old Bussen, we are able to say, and it makes us feel better, more secure, in our own fortune. Sometimes there are worse things than cold and hunger. Had you thought of that? Do you know him at all, his feelings, or his plan for himself? I think until you do, don't interfere."

"If we hadn't interfered today, he might be dead by now," said Charles.

"We may have made a mistake even so," said Tadeusz, calmly. "Now we must wait and see. Of course if we could give him money or food without letting him know why we did it, that would be another thing. But we can't. If you go now after all that has happened and offer him a coat, just like that, why, what can you expect? He would feel like throwing it back at you. A man might accept charity if he did not fear the contempt of the giver. But only good friends can accept or exchange favors. Otherwise it doesn't do." Tadeusz stood up and walked about quickly, bent at the waist and peering at Charles. "Dear fellow, don't mind if I say, you Americans have some very odd notions. Why all this benevolence? What do you expect to gain by it?

Charles said, "I wouldn't gain anything by it, and I would expect to lose a coat. But I don't need the coat," he said, "and so far as I am concerned that would be the end of it."

"You sound morally indignant," said Tadeusz. He paused before Charles and smiled. "Don't get mad, you hear how well I speak American? You would gain from it the pride in being able to give a coat. And Herr Bussen would be warm, but he would owe his coat to the charity of a stranger, and it might spoil his whole career. Try to understand. I know more about this than you do. If ever I come to your country I will take your advice about Americans."

"I don't believe Americans are so different from other people as all that," said Charles.

"Believe me," said Tadeusz, "you are like beings from another planet to us. Don't offer a coat to Herr Bussen. He will hate you for it."

Charles said, "I can't believe it really."

"If you set yourself up as a benefactor," said Tadeusz,

"you must expect to be hated. Let me tell you something. A very rich man I know wished to give good sums of money to help young musicians. But he went to his lawyer and insisted that the gift must be anonymous; under no circumstances must the giver be known. Well, the lawyer said of course it would be arranged, but it would make work, mystery, why did his client want that? And this very wise man said, 'I am superstitious and I do not want them to be able to curse me by name.' "

"Good God," said Charles, sincerely horrified.

"Ah, yes, good God," said Tadeusz, amiably.

Charles left the coat in his closet, and brought milk and oranges instead to Herr Bussen. Hans was there already, sitting besides the bed offering Herr Bussen more soup.

The invalid accepted, and swallowed the nourishment as if it were bitter medicine. Charles thought, Yes, it's true, he isn't getting any good out of it; and he saw plainly that Herr Bussen felt himself being engulfed slowly in a debt he had no hope of paying. Charles, at the foot of the bed, had a curious scene flash through his mind: Herr Bussen, the object of charity, fleeing like a stag across the snowy waste, with Hans and Tadeusz and Rosa and he, Charles, after him in full cry, bringing him down, by the throat if necessary, to give him aid and comfort. Charles heard the deep mournful voices of his father's liver-spotted hounds.

✦

When Rosa brought the coffee tray, one end of it was occupied by an ordinary looking black japanned metal box. She stood, without pouring the coffee, her hands on the table, and said in a low voice, "This hasn't been a very good day for anybody, I suppose. But I have on my conscience my sharpness to Herr Bussen. I have told him so, and he answered—he answered kindly," she said. "But I know that you, a stranger, and from a rich country—"

"The country may be rich," said Charles, "but most of the people in it are not—"

"Couldn't be expected to understand," Rosa went on, waving his speech away without listening. "Look, I want to show you something, then maybe you will see a little of what has happened to us. Outlanders, all the world, come here with their money—"

"I tell you I am not rich, for one," said Charles, hopelessly. She gave him a stare very much like contempt for his lying speech; she knew better. He was the worst kind of rich American, the kind who pretended to be poor. "With their money," she said, angrily, raising her voice, "and then they think we are cheap because we worry about how we shall live. You despise us because we are ruined and why are we ruined, tell me that? It is because your country deserted and betrayed us in the war, you should have helped us and you did not." Her voice dropped and became bitter and quiet.

Charles said in a matter-of-fact, reasoning tone: "All the way over on the boat, the Germans kept telling me that. The truth is, I've heard talk about that war all my life, but I hardly remember it. I have to confess I hadn't thought much about it. If I had, maybe I would never have come here."

"You didn't have to think about it," said Rosa, "but here, we have nothing else to think about." She opened the black box. It was full of paper money, thick bales of it in rubber bands, such an amount of printed money as Charles had seen only in glimpses at the elbow of a clerk behind the barred windows of a great bank. Rosa lifted one of the bundles.

"These are nothing," she said with affected airiness, "these are only a hundred thousand marks each. . . . Wait." She lifted another and flirted the edges through her fingers. "These are five hundred thousand marks each—look," she said, her voice wavering. "One million marks each, these." She dropped each bundle as she spoke upon the table beside them without glancing up. Terror and awe were in her face, as if again for just a moment, she believed in the value of this paper as she had once believed. "Did you ever see a note for five million marks? Here are a hundred of them, you will never see this again—and oh," she cried suddenly, in a frenzy of grief, clutching the treacherous stuff with both hands, "try now to buy a loaf of bread with all this, try it, try it!"

Her voice rose and she wept shamelessly without hiding

her face, her arms hanging loosely, the worthless money dropping to the floor.

Charles looked about as if he expected help, rescue, to come by miracle. He backed away from her thinking only of escape, saying as well as he could, "I know it is all a horrible business—but, what can I do?"

This dull question had a remarkable effect. Rosa's tears dried almost instantly, her voice deepened a note, she spoke with intense anger. "You can do nothing," she said vehemently, "nothing, you know nothing at all, you cannot even imagine—"

Charles picked up the money from the carpet, and Rosa began placing the stiff pale colored bundles again in the box, carefully, arranging them first one way and another, stopping now and then to squeeze the end of her nose with her thin little handkerchief. "Nothing to say, nothing to be done," she repeated, giving him a resentful look as if he had failed her, a look as personal and angry as if she were a member of his family, or at least a familiar friend, or—what on earth was Rosa to him? A middle-aged stranger who had rented him a room, someone he had expected to see and speak to perhaps once a week, and here she was, swarming all over him, weeping on his neck, telling her troubles, putting the blame for the troubles on the world on him, driving him nuts, and no way that he could see of getting out of it. She closed the box and leaned her hands on the table. "When you are so poor," she said, "you are frightened of the poor and unfortunate. I was frightened of Herr Bussen—no, I almost hated him. I thought every day, 'My God, such a man will bring bad luck on us all, he will drag us all down with him.' " She spoke in a very low tone. "But today, it came to me that Herr Bussen will live through everything, he is strong, he is not really afraid. And that is a comfort to me, because I am afraid of everything."

She poured the coffee, took up the japanned box and went out.

The household settled down that night for a good sleep. What a relief, thought Charles, to put a long quiet stretch of darkness between you and the thing that happened. Suppose Old Bussen had popped off? He felt warmly towards Old Bussen, who was still breathing—snoring, in fact, in long rich groans, as if he couldn't breathe hard enough.

When Charles put his head in to look at Herr Bussen the next morning, two rawboned solemn youths with identical leather-colored forelocks were sitting with him, one on the bed, one on the spindling chair. They turned and gazed at the stranger with profound blue eyes exactly alike, and Herr Bussen, looking very well and merry, introduced them. Twin brothers, he said, school friends of his, who were at that moment on the point of fulfilling a life's ambition. On New Year's Eve they were going to open a small cabaret of their own, a snug little half-cellar with the best beer, a supper table and pretty girls who could sing and dance. Nothing big, but a good place, and Herr Bussen hoped Charles would go with him to celebrate the first evening. Charles said it sounded a fine idea to him, and thought perhaps Hans and Tadeusz would like to go, too. The brothers eyed him without a flicker of expression.

Herr Bussen sat up as if he had new life in him. "Oh, yes, we will all go together." The brothers stood up to giant heights, and one of them said, "It will not be expensive, either." As if being able to give this piece of good news was pleasant to him, he grinned broadly and reassuringly at Charles, who grinned in turn. He said to Herr Bussen, "I'm going out. Could I bring you anything?"

"Oh, no," said Herr Bussen, firmly, shaking his head with a small glitter of resentment in his eye. "Thank you, nothing at all. I'm getting up now."

At the foot of the shallow flight of steps leading to the new cabaret, a dish of food scraps had been set out for the hungry small animals. A black cat was there, eating very fast, glancing nervously over his shoulder as he swallowed. One of the twins put his head out, invited his four visitors in festively, noticed the cat and said ritually, "May it do him good." He threw open the door to disclose a small, freshly painted, well lighted little place, full of tables covered with red checkerboard cloths, a modest bar, and at the farther end, a long table set out with cold supper. It could all be seen at a glance. There was a homemade air about the colored paper decorations, the feathery tinsel draped above the bar mirror, the rack full of steins and the small cuckoo clock.

It was hardly Charles' notion of a Berlin cabaret; he had heard about Berlin night life and expected something more sophisticated. He remarked as much to Tadeusz.

"Oh, no," said Tadeusz, "this is another kind of thing altogether. This is going to be nice-stuffy-middle-class-German full of rosy emotions and beer. You could bring your most innocent child here if you had an innocent child." He seemed pleased, and so did Hans and Herr Bussen: they walked about and praised everything the brothers had done. All of them were pleasantly excited because none of them had ever known anyone who ran a cabaret, and they enjoyed a cozy feeling of being on the inside of things for once. Almost immediately they began calling Herr Bussen by his first name. Tadeusz began it.

"Otto, dear fellow, could you give me a light?" he asked, and Otto, who did not smoke, blushed with pleasure and felt in his pockets as if he expected to find matches.

They were the first comers. As the brothers went on about their last-minute business, rushing back and forth through the swinging door leading to the kitchen, Otto led the way to the supper table, where they helped themselves comfortably but carefully, for at close range there was an air of thrift about the food, as if the cheese and sausages had been counted and the bread weighed, perhaps. A boy in a white jacket brought them tall steins of beer; they lifted them to each other, waved them at the brothers, and drank long and deeply.

"In Munich," said Tadeusz, "I used to drink with a crowd of music students, all Germans. We drank and drank, and the man who had to leave the table first paid for all. I always paid. It was a bore, really."

"A dull custom at best," commented Hans, "and of course the kind of thing foreigners would notice and tell about, as if it were typical." His face was quietly annoyed, he looked past Tadeusz, who refused to be snubbed.

"I have already agreed with you it was a bore," he said, "and after all, only an incident of life in Munich." His tone was soothing, indulgent, a little insolent. Charles, observing, thought with some slight surprise that these fellows did not like each other, after all. And almost instantly he felt indifference tinged with dislike for them both, and an uneasy feeling that he was in the wrong company; he wished pretty thoroughly he had not come to that place with them.

One of the brothers leaned over them with his open, single-minded expression, calling their attention to newcomers. A stupidly handsome young man with a careful thatch of curls above a self-consciously god-like brow was helping an olive-skinned, yellow-haired young woman with her wraps. "A star in the moving pictures," whispered the brother, excitedly, "and that girl is his mistress and his leading lady." He dived towards his celebrities awkwardly, saw them settled and was back in a moment. "There comes Lutte, a model, one of the most beautiful girls in Berlin," he said, his voice throbbing. "She is going to dance a rumba when the time comes."

They all turned in natural curiosity and saw indeed a very beautiful slender girl, her head shining like a silver yellow peony above her rather skimpy black dress. She smiled and waved her hand at them, they stood up and bowed, but she did not approach them as they had hoped. Leaning on the bar, she talked to the boy in the white jacket. The room filled then rather rapidly, there was a rush for the long table and the brothers, flushed with success, beamed and scurried with trays and steins. A small orchestra moved into the space beside the bar.

Almost every guest, Charles noticed, had brought a musical instrument, a violin or flute or white piano accordion, a clarinet; and one man lumbered in under the burden of a violoncello in a green baize-covered case. A young woman with huge haunches and thick legs, a knot of sleek brown hair slipping upon her unpowdered neck, came in by herself, looked around with a vague smile which no one returned, and went behind the bar, where she began competently to set up trays of beer.

"There you see her," said Hans, looking at Lutte possessively, "the truest type of German beauty—tell me, have you seen anything better anywhere?"

"Oh, come now," said Tadeusz, mildly, "there aren't a half dozen like her in this town. The legs and feet, surely they aren't typical? She might have French blood, or even a little Polish," he said. "Only she is perhaps a little flat-bosomed for that."

"What you seem never to understand," said Hans, in a slightly edged voice, "is that when I say German I don't mean peasants or these fat Berliners."

"Perhaps we should always mean peasants when we speak of a race," said Tadeusz. "The nobility and the royalty are always mixed bloods, the complete mongrel, really, they have no nationality at all. Even the middle classes marry everywhere, but the peasant stays in his own region and marries his own kind, generation after generation, and creates the race, quite simply, as I see it."

"The trouble with that notion," said Hans, "is that the peasantry of almost any country looks quite like the peasantry of any other."

"Oh, superficially," said Otto. "Their heads are very different, if you will study them." He leaned forward earnestly. "No matter how it came about," he told them, "the true great old Germanic type is lean and tall and fair as gods." His forehead formed a deep wrinkle which sank to a meaty cleft between his brows. His small puffy eyes swam tenderly, the roll of fat across his collar flushed with emotion. "We are not by any means all the pig type," he said humbly, spreading his thick hands, "though I know the foreign caricaturists make us all appear so. Those were perhaps the old Wendish people, and after all, they were a single tribe, they are not of the old true great Germanic—"

"Type," finished Tadeusz, mildly rude. "Let's agree then, the Germans are all of the highest type of beauty and they have preposterously fine manners. Look at all the heel-clicking and bowing from the waist and elegant high-toned voices. And how polite and smiling a seven-foot policeman can be when he is getting ready to crack your skull open. I have seen it. No, Hans, you have a great culture here, no doubt, but I think no civilization. You will be the last race on earth to be civilized, but does it matter?"

"On the other hand," said Hans with extreme politeness, smiling, a cold gleam in his eye, "the Poles, if you like that high-cheeked, low-browed Tartar style, have also great physical beauty, and though they have contributed exactly nothing to world-culture, they are civilized in a medieval sort of way, I suppose."

"Thanks," said Tadeusz, turning towards Hans as if to show his flat cheeks and narrow high forehead. "One of my grandmothers was a Tartar, and you can see how typical I am."

"One of your grandfathers was an Austrian, too," said Otto; "I'd never think of you as a Pole. You seem to me an Austrian."

"Oh, by God, I can't have that," said Tadeusz, decidedly, and he laughed with his lips tightly closed. "No, no, I'll be a Tartar first. But I am a Pole just the same."

Charles had never seen any Poles except a few short-legged broad-faced men laying railroad ties somewhere in the South, and he would not have known they were Poles unless someone had told him, and the man called them Polacks, besides. He could make nothing of Tadeusz, but Hans and Otto both seemed persons he had known before; Texas was full of boys like Otto, and Hans reminded him of Kuno. It seemed to him that the discussion was getting nowhere, and it reminded him of quarrels during his schooldays between the German boys and Mexican boys and the Kentucky boys; the Irish boys fought everybody, and Charles, who was partly Irish, remembered that he had done a good deal of fighting in which all sight of the original dispute had been lost in the simple love of violence. He said, "All the way over on the boat the Germans kept telling me I was not a typical American. How could they know? Of course I am perfectly typical."

"Oh, not at all," said Tadeusz, and this time his good humor was real. "We know all about you. Americans are all cowboys or very rich, and when they are rich they get drunk in poor countries and paste thousand-franc notes on their suitcases, or light cigarettes with them—"

"Oh, God," said Charles simply. "Who started that story?" Even American tourists went about repeating it with complacent horror, as if to prove they were not that sort of tourist.

"You know what is the trouble?" asked Tadeusz, amiably. "The Americans we know are all so filthy rich. There is nothing Europeans love and crave and covet more than wealth. If we didn't believe your country has all the money, there would be nothing wrong with you, particularly."

"We're punch drunk, anyhow," said Charles. "We don't give a damn any more."

"Europeans hate each other for everything and for nothing; they've been trying to destroy each other for two thousand years, why do you Americans expect us to like you?" asked Tadeusz.

"We don't expect it," said Charles. "Who said we did? We, naturally, like just everybody. We are sentimental. Just like the Germans. You want to be loved for yourselves alone and you are always right and you can never see why other people can't see you in the same rosy light you see yourselves. Look what a glorious people you are and yet nobody loves you. Well, that's a great pity."

Otto gazed earnestly at Charles from under his deep brows, wagged his head and said, "I do not think you really like anybody, you Americans. You are indifferent to everybody and so it is easy for you to be gay, to be careless, to seem friendly. You are really a coldhearted indifferent people. You have no troubles. You have no troubles because you do not know how to have them. Even if you get troubles, you think it is just a package meant for the people next door, delivered to you by mistake. That is what I really believe."

Charles, embittered, said, "I can't talk about whole countries because I never knew one, not even my own. I only know a few persons here and there and some I like and some I don't like and I never thought it anything but a personal matter. . . ."

Tadeusz said, "Oh, dear fellow, that is being much too modest. The whole art of self-importance is to raise your personal likes and dislikes to the plane of moral or esthetic principle, and to apply on an international scale your smallest personal experience. . . . If someone steps on your foot, you should not rest until you have raised an army to avenge you. . . . And as for us, what are we doing with our evening? At this rate I shall have indigestion. . . ."

"What about our friends the French?" asked Hans, suddenly. "Can anyone find fault with them? Their food, their wine, their dress, their manners—" he lifted his stein and drank without enjoyment, and added—"a race of monkeys."

"They have very bad manners," said Tadeusz, "and they would cut you into ribbons with a dull pair of scissors for five francs in hand. A shortsighted and selfish people, and how I love them. But not as I do the English. Take the English—"

"Take the Italians," said Charles, "all of them."

"Nothing worth mentioning since Dante," said Tadeusz. "I detest their lumpy Renaissance."

"Now that's settled," said Charles, "let's take the pigmies, or the Icelanders, or the head hunters of Borneo—"

"I love them all," cried Tadeusz, "especially the Irish. I like the Irish because they are nearly as damnation patriotic as the Poles."

"I was brought up on Irish patriotism," said Charles. "My mother's name was O'Hara, and I was supposed to be proud of it, but you have a tough time being proud if you are called Harp and Potato Mouth at school where the others are all Scotch Presbyterians or of English descent."

Tadeusz said, "What nonsense," and he began to talk pleasantly and quietly about the great ancient Celtic race, slyly too, aiming at Hans; praising their ancient culture of which traces were found in all parts of Europe. "Yes, even the Germans have been improved by it," he said. Hans and Otto shook their heads, but their anger seemed to have disappeared, their faces smoothed and their eyes met openly once more. Charles was soothed and flattered to find Irish greatness acknowledged at last by somebody other than his immediate family. He said to Tadeusz, "My father used to tell me, 'Ah, the Irish, my boy. God knows they went down early in time, but don't forget this, they had a great national culture when the British were still painting themselves blue, and the old French used to exchange scholars with them!' "

Tadeusz translated this to Hans and Otto, and Hans laughed so suddenly he put his hand to his cheek with a grimace. "Be careful," said Tadeusz, looking at the wound as he always did, with an air of clinical interest, which he knew Hans liked. Charles went on to say he had never seen such a statement in any history books, which seemed very vague about the Irish until they began fighting with the British. By that time, the books said in effect, they were just a lot of wild bog-jumpers. He had felt sorry for his father, trying to wring a drop of comfort out of the myth of his splendid past, but the usual run of histories on the subject hadn't borne him out. He was pleased to think he had simply got hold of the wrong books.

"They are very like the Poles," said Tadeusz, "those Irish, living on the glory of their past, on their poetry and the jeweled Book of Kells and the great cups and crowns of ancient Ireland, the memories of victories and defeats godlike in intensity, the hope of rising again to glory: and in the meantime," he added, "always fighting quite a lot and very unsuccessfully."

Hans leaned forward and spoke with importance, as if he

were a professor addressing his class: "The fate of Ireland (and of Poland, too, Tadeusz, don't forget) is an example, a most terrible example, of what can happen to a country when it divides against itself and lets the enemy in . . . the Irish, so nationalistic at this late day, are yet divided. What do they expect? They could have saved themselves in early time by uniting and attacking the enemy, instead of waiting to be attacked."

Tadeusz reminded him, "Hans, that does not always work either," but Hans ignored the little gibe.

Charles, ill-informed as he was, floundering in the quicksands of popular history, could not answer, yet the whole notion was offensive to him. "But why jump on a man unless he jumps first?"

Hans, the youthful oracle, was ready. "Why, because he always attacks when you are not looking, or when you have put down your arms for an instant. So you are punished for carelessness really, for not troubling to learn the intentions of your enemy. You are beaten, and that is the end of you, unless you can gather strength and fight again."

"The Celts aren't ended," said Tadeusz; "they exist in great numbers and are scattered all over and still have influence everywhere they touch."

"Influence?" asked Hans. "A purely oblique, feminine, worthless thing, influence. Power, pure power is what counts to a nation or a race. You must be able to tell other peoples what to do, and above all what they may not do, you must be able to enforce every order you give against no matter what opposition, and when you demand anything at all, it must be given you without question. That is the only power, and power is the only thing of any value or importance in this world."

"It doesn't last, though, any better than some other things," said Tadeusz. "It doesn't always work as well as long ruse and intelligent strategy. It goes down in the long run."

"Maybe it goes down because powerful people get tired of power," said Otto, leaning his head on his hand and looking discouraged; "maybe they wear themselves out beating other people and spying on them and ordering them about and robbing them. Maybe they exhaust themselves."

"And maybe one day they overstep themselves, or a new young power rises to put an end to them," said Tadeusz; "that happens."

"Maybe they find out it doesn't pay," said Charles.

"It always pays," said Hans; "that is the point. It pays, and nothing else does. Everything else is childish beside it. Otto, you surprise me. That is a strange point of view for you."

Otto sagged, guilty and uncomfortable. "I am not a soldier," he said. "I love study and quiet."

Hans sat very stiffly, an alienated hostile glitter in his eyes. He turned halfway to Charles and said, "We Germans were beaten in the last war, thanks partly to your great country, but we shall win in the next."

A chill ran down Charles' spine, he shrugged his shoulders. They were all a little drunk, there might be a row if they didn't pull themselves together. He did not want to quarrel with anybody, nor to fight the war over again. "We were all in short pants when that war was ended," he said. Hans answered instantly, "Ah, yes, but we will all be in uniforms for the next."

Tadeusz said, "Oh, come now, dear Hans, I never felt less bloodthirsty in my life. I only want to play the piano."

"I want to paint," said Charles.

"I want to teach mathematics," said Otto.

"Neither am I bloodthirsty," said Hans, "but I know what will happen." His cheek, under its band of court plaster, was slightly more swollen than earlier in the evening. The fingers of his left hand explored tenderly along the line of angry blue flesh. He said, in a bright impersonal tone, "Look, it is most interesting to remember one thing. We should have won that war, and we lost it in the first three days, though we did not know it, or could not believe it, for four years. What was the cause? One single delayed order, one sole failure of a body of troops to move at a given moment, on that first advance through Belgium. A delay of three days lost us that war. Well, it won't happen the next time."

"No," said Tadeusz, gently, "the next time, there will be

another kind of mistake, something else quite different will go wrong, who knows how or why? It is always like that. Wars are not won by intelligence, Hans. Can't you see that? All the fine planning in the world can't insure an army against that one fellow who will, when the moment comes, delay, or give the wrong order, or be in the wrong place. Why, the other side did nothing but blunder all the way through, and yet they won, that time."

"Sea power," said Charles, "good old sea power. I bet on that. It wins in the long run."

"Carthage was a sea power, but she didn't beat Rome," said Otto.

"The next time," said Hans, with cool stubbornness, "they won't win. You'll see. The next time, there will be no mistakes on our side."

"I can wait," said Tadeusz, "I am in no hurry."

"I can wait, all right," said Charles, "and meantime, let me get the beer."

The orchestra, increased by the efforts of guests with their fiddles, flutes and the violoncello, had been making a fine din, so that the four voices had been rising gradually. "Let's give it up for the present," said Tadeusz; "it can't be settled this evening."

The actor and his mistress were gone, and Lutte remained the only beauty in the room. She was sitting with several young men and another girl at a table near by, all drinking beer heartily, laughing constantly and falling into each other's arms at intervals for embraces and smacks on the cheek, the boys kissing boys or girls alike with indiscriminate warmth. Lutte caught Charles' glance and waved her beer glass at him. He waved back and smiled excitedly. She was a knockout and he hoped quite violently to know her better. And even at that moment, like the first symptoms of some fatal sickness, there stirred in him a most awful premonition of disaster, and his thoughts, blurred with drink and strangeness and the sound of half-understood tongues and the climate of remembered wrongs and hatreds, revolved dimly around vague remembered tales of Napoleon and Genghis Khan and Attila the Hun and all the Caesars and Alexander the Great and Darius and the dim Pharaohs and lost Babylon. He felt helpless, undefended, looked at the three strange faces near him and decided not to drink any more, for he must not be drunker than they; he trusted none of them.

Otto, leaving his beer, wandered away, and one of the brothers handed him a white piano accordion as he passed. The change in Otto was miraculous. From soggy gloom his face turned to a great mask of simple enjoyment, he took up the tune the orchestra was playing and roamed among the tables, the instrument folding and unfolding in his arms, his blunt fingers flying over the keys. In a fine roaring voice he began to sing:

"Ich armes welsches Teufelein
Ich kann nicht mehr marschieren–"

"MARSCHIEREN!" roared every voice in the place, joyously. "Ich kann nicht mehr marschier'n."

Otto sang: "Ich hab' verlor'n mein Pfeiflein
Aus meinen Mantelsack–"

" 'SACK!" yelled the chorus, "Aus meinen Mantelsack."

Hans stood up and sang in a clear light voice: "Ich hab', ich hab' gefunden, was du verloren hast–"

"HAST!" bawled the chorus, and everybody was standing now, their laughing faces innocent and pure as lambs at play, "was du verloren hast."

There was a great wave of laughter after this, and the orchestra suddenly changed to "The Peanut Vendor." Lutte, with a serious face as if she were fulfilling her duty, stood up and began to dance alone, something supposed no doubt to be a rumba, but to Charles, it seemed rather a combination of the black bottom and the hoochy-coochy such as he had seen, sneaking off furtively with other boys, in carnival side-shows during his innocent boyhood in Texas. He had danced the rumba to the tune of "The Peanut Vendor" all the way from his home town, across the Atlantic and straight into Bremen harbor, and it occurred to him that here was something he could really do. He took the gourds from the quiet little fellow who was clacking them rather feebly, and began to do his version of the rumba, shaking the gourds and cracking them together with great authority.

He could hear hands clapping in rhythm all over the room, and Lutte, abandoning her solo, began to dance with him. He handed back the gourds at once and took Lutte firmly around her warm, agitated waist, very thinly covered. She held her face back from him stiffly, smiled with a fair imitation of a cinematic *femme fatale*, and rather clumsily but with great meaning bumped her hip against him. He gathered her in, folded her up to him as close as he could, but she stiffened again and bumped him, this time full in the stomach. "What say we give up the technique and let nature take its course," said Charles, with a straight face.

"What is that?" she asked, unexpectedly in English. "I do not understand."

"Well," said Charles, kissing her on the cheek, "it speaks English too." She did not kiss back, but went limp and began to dance naturally.

"Am I as beautiful as that moving picture actress who was here this evening?" asked Lutte, wistfully.

"At least," said Charles.

"Would I do for the moving pictures in America, in your Hollywood?" she asked, leaning upon him.

"Don't bump," said Charles. "Yes, you would do fine in Hollywood."

"Do I dance well enough?" asked Lutte.

"Yes, darling, you do. You are a whizz."

"What is that?"

"Something wonderful," said Charles. "Come to me, angel."

"Do you know anybody in Hollywood?" asked Lutte, sticking firmly to her one interest.

"No, but you might," said Charles; "all Germany and Central Europe are there already; you'd be bound to run into friends. Anyway you won't be lonesome long."

Lutte put her mouth like a ripe peach to his ear and blowing warmly upon it whispered, "Take me to America with you."

"Let's go," said Charles, and seizing her more firmly he ran a few steps towards the door. She held back. "No, I am serious, I want to go to America."

"So do I," said Charles, recklessly, "so does everybody."

"That is not true," said Lutte, severely, almost stopping in her tracks. At this moment Hans cut in. Charles sat down feeling cheated. Lutte's manner changed completely. She melted towards Hans, they danced slowly and as they danced, she kissed him softly and continually and gently on his right cheek, her mouth meek and sweet, her eyes nearly closed. Over Hans' disfigured face came that same look of full-fed pride, of composed self-approval—of arrogance, that was the word. Charles felt a flicker of sharp hatred for Hans. Then it passed. "Hell," he said, aloud, yet to no one, "what of it?"

"I think so too," said Tadeusz, "I think, hell, what of it?"

"Let's have some brandy," said Charles. Otto was sitting quietly, he roused and smiled.

"What a fine evening!" he said. "We are all friends, are we not?"

"Completely," said Tadeusz, "we are all friends to you, Otto." He had grown quieter and softer in his gestures, his eyes peered vaguely between his wrinkled lids, his little tight smile was constant. "I am getting damnation drunk, and my conscience will begin hurting soon," he said, contentedly. Then the others, listening dimly, heard him telling some story about his childhood in Cracow. ". . . in the old house where my family have lived since the twelfth century . . ." he said. "At Easter we ate only pork in contempt of the Jews, and after the long fasting of Lent naturally we gorged ourselves shamelessly. . . . On Easter morning after High Mass I would eat until I was perfectly round, and in pain. Then I would lie down and cry, and when they asked me what troubled me, I would say, out of shame, that my conscience was hurting me. They would be very respectful and comfort me, but sometimes I thought I saw a gleam in an eye, or just a flash of a look on a face—not my mother's, but my sister's, perhaps—she was a horrid, knowing little thing—and my nurse's. One day my nurse gave me some soothing syrup and rubbed my stomach with that insulting false sympathy and said, 'There now, your conscience feels better, doesn't it?' I went howling and told my mother that my nurse had kicked me in the stomach. Then I upchucked all my Easter pork, so the Jews had their revenge for once. My nurse said, 'What a little monster it is'; then she and my mother talked in the next room, and when they came back smiling I knew the game was up. I never mentioned my conscience again to them. But once after I was grown up, or nearly, I was very drunk and came home at four in the morning, and I crawled upstairs because it seemed unreasonable, this business of people walking about on their hind legs all the time. The red stair carpet gave me a sense of great security and ease, and I remember feeling that I was a kind of prophet of good for mankind, restoring an old way of locomotion which would probably revolutionize all society once I had proved its pleasures and possibilities. The first obstacle I encountered was my mother. She stood at the head of the stairs holding a lighted candle, waiting without a word. I waved one paw at her but she did not respond. And when I put my head above the last step she kicked me under the chin and almost knocked me out. She never mentioned this incident and I could hardly believe it myself except for my sore tongue the next day. Well, such was my upbringing in that old city, but I remember it dearly now, something between a cemetery and a Lost Paradise, with an immense sound of bells. . . ."

Otto said, "Maybe we should have some beer," and with a sad mouth he talked a little about his own childhood. His mother had beaten him quite hard one day, without warning, when he was cracking walnuts and eating them. With tears he had asked her why, and she said, "Don't ask me any questions. What is good enough for Martin Luther is good enough for you." And later in a child's book he had read how Luther's mother had beaten him until the blood came because he annoyed her with the sound of cracking nuts. "Until then I had thought of Luther as a great, forbidding cruel man who loved bloodshed, but after that I felt sorry for him. He was once a poor helpless child like me, beaten for nothing," Otto said, "and yet he became great." His face was full of humble apology. "That was child's nonsense, but it helped me to live," he said.

The drifting smoke and the lights and the voices and the music were all mingled and swimming together around their heads. The big young woman who had been helping at the bar came then, her knot of hair slipping still further down her neck, and seemed to be pulling chairs and tables towards the wall. Her fine haunches jiggled under her tight skirt, her great breasts were stretching and falling as she raised and lowered her arms, her heavy legs were braced far apart as she pushed at a table. The men sitting about watched her without moving or offering help. Charles observed another change in Otto. He was watching the girl intently, his mouth moistening. He seemed lost in a pleasant daze, his nose twitched, his eyes grew round and took on the calculating ferocity of a tomcat's. The girl leaned over and the hollows of her knees showed; she straightened up and the muscles of her back and shoulders writhed. Slowly, feeling Otto's gaze upon her, she began to blush. Her neck turned red, her cheeks, her forehead, the whole face stiffened and darkened as if she were resisting pain, or a surge of anger. But the corners of her soft formless mouth were smiling, and she did not raise her eyes again after her first quick glance. Quite suddenly she gave a last plunge at a chair, set it in place with a thump, and ran away, her body full of awkward, contradictory motions. Otto turned to Charles, and showered upon him the remains of his impassioned gaze at the girl.

"There is a fine armful for you," he said; "I like big strong girls." Charles nodded as if he agreed, and looked again at Lutte, still dancing with Hans and kissing him.

A wooden cuckoo about the size of a humming bird leaped from his little door above the clockface and began his warning note. Instantly everybody rose and each one embraced the person nearest him, shouting, "Happy New Year, health, good luck, happy New Year, God bless you." Glasses and steins danced aloft in half circles, spilling foam on uplifted faces. A disordered circle formed, arms interlocked, and a ragged singing began which smoothed out almost at once into a deep chorus, the fine voices swinging along together in frolicsome tunes Charles did not know. He swayed with the circle, woven into it, he opened his mouth and sang tunelessly without words. Real joy, warm and careless, swept him away; this was a place to be, these were wonderful people, he liked absolutely everybody there. The circle broke up, ran together, whirled, loosened, fell apart.

Hans came over smiling on one side of his face, Lutte beside him. They put their arms around Charles together and wished him a happy New Year. He stood there swaying with an arm around each, all jealousy gone. Lutte kissed him sweetly on the mouth, and he kissed back but like a child. Then they all saw Tadeusz leaning over Otto, who was sprawled at the little table, head pillowed on his arms.

"He's gone completely, he has deserted us," said Tadeusz. "Now we must drag him about with us wherever we go for the rest of the evening."

"We aren't going anywhere else, are we," asked Charles, "for God's sake?"

Otto was indeed gone, altogether. They got him up by the arms, and in a busy sort of scramble they found themselves on the sidewalk, with a tall policeman watching mildly, getting into a taxicab, where their feet were tangled hopelessly and they all seemed to hang at once dangerously far out of the windows. Lutte was saying, to all of them alike, "Good night, happy New Year," her face shining but sober looking.

On the staircase, Otto collapsed once for all. The three pulled him along slowly, pausing at every step. At moments the whole structure tottered, they would stagger and lose hold of each other and step on Otto, who groaned and howled, but without resentment. They would heave themselves together more firmly and start again, making wild sounds of laughter, nodding at each other as if agreed on some inexplicable but gloriously comic truth. "Let's crawl," shouted Charles to Tadeusz; "maybe it will work this time." Hans disapproved of this instantly.

"No crawling," he said, taking command at once. "Every man goes up on his own feet, except perhaps Otto." They assembled themselves once more for a last effort, and arrived at the door known to be theirs.

Rosa's door was ajar slightly, a streak of light shining into the hall. They regarded it with sobering gloom, expecting the door to fly open and Rosa to rush forth scolding. Nothing happened. They changed their tactics, and dragging Otto, they rushed her door, beating on it in tattoo and shouting recklessly, "Happy New Year, Roslein, Roslein, happy New Year."

There was a small flurry inside, the door opened a few inches more, and Rosa put out a sleek, orderly head. Her eyes were a little pink and sleepy looking, but she was smiling a gay, foxy smile. Her pensioners were most lordly drunk, she saw at a glance, none the worse for it, thank God. Hans' cheek was discolored somewhat more, but he was laughing, Charles and Tadeusz were quieter, trying to appear sober and responsible, but their eyelids drooped, they leered drolly. The three were supporting Herr Bussen between them, and Herr Bussen, hanging at random, his knees bent, had a blissful innocent confidence in his sleeping face.

"Happy New Year, you owls," said Rosa, proud of her household who knew how to celebrate an occasion. "I had champagne too, with friends, and New Year's punch. I am a little merry too," she told them, boasting. "Go to sleep now, look, this is the New Year. You must start it well tomorrow. Good night."

Charles sat on the feather bed and wriggled out of his clothes, pushing them off any old way and leaving them where they fell. As he fumbled with his pajamas, his eyes swam about in his head, seeing first one thing and then another, but none of it familiar, nothing that was his. He did notice at last that the Leaning Tower seemed to be back, sitting now safely behind the glass of the corner cabinet. By a roundabout way he brought himself across the room to the Tower. It was there, all right, and it was mended pretty obviously, it would never be the same. But for Rosa, poor old woman, he supposed it was better than nothing. It stood for something she had, or thought she had, once. Even all patched up as it was, and worthless to begin with, it meant something to her, and he was still ashamed of having broken it; it made him feel like a heel. It stood there in its bold little frailness, as if daring him to come on; how well he knew that a thumb and forefinger would smash the thin ribs, the mended spots would fall at a breath. Leaning, suspended, perpetually ready to fall but never falling quite, the venturesome little object—a mistake in the first place, a whimsical pain in the neck, really, towers shouldn't lean in the first place; a curiosity, like those cupids falling off the roof—yet had some kind of meaning in Charles' mind. Well, what? He tousled his hair and rubbed his eyes and then his whole head and yawned himself almost inside out. What had the silly little thing reminded him of before? There was an answer if he could think what it was, but this was not the time. But just the same, there was something terribly urgent at work, in him or around him, he could not tell which. There was something perishable but threatening, uneasy, hanging over his head or stirring angrily, dangerously, at his back. If he couldn't find out now what it was that troubled him so in this place, maybe he would never know. He stood there feeling his drunkenness as a pain and a weight on him, unable to think clearly but feeling what he had never known before, an infernal desolation of the spirit, the chill and the knowledge of death in him. He wrapped his arms across his chest and expelled his breath, and a cold sweat broke out all over him. He went towards the bed and fell upon it and rolled himself into a knot, being rather unpleasant with himself. "All you need is a crying jag to make it complete," he said. But he didn't feel sorry for himself, and no crying jag or any other kind of jag would ever, in this world, do anything at all for him.